the
Prince of
WISDOM

the Prince of WISDOM

R.C. JONES

Ambassador International
GREENVILLE, SOUTH CAROLINA & BELFAST, NORTHERN IRELAND

www.ambassador-international.com

The Prince of Wisdom

© 2019 by R.C. Jones
All rights reserved

ISBN: 978-1-62020-972-1
eISBN: 978-1-62020-988-2

Scripture taken from the New King James Version®. Copyright © 1982 by Thomas Nelson. Used by permission. All rights reserved.

Cover Design & Typesetting by Hannah Nichols
Ebook Conversion by Anna Riebe Raats

AMBASSADOR INTERNATIONAL
Emerald House
411 University Ridge, Suite B14
Greenville, SC 29601, USA
www.ambassador-international.com

AMBASSADOR BOOKS
The Mount
2 Woodstock Link
Belfast, BT6 8DD, Northern Ireland, UK
www.ambassadormedia.co.uk

The colophon is a trademark of Ambassador, a Christian publishing company.

Behold, I send you out as sheep in the midst of wolves. Therefore be wise as serpents and harmless as doves.

—Matthew 10:16

Once upon a time, in a mystical land far, far away, there was an amazing kingdom called Eskolar. Everything about the kingdom was great: from its glittering buildings, to its fantastic traditions, and its amazing people. Everything in Eskolar was simply spectacular.

But the kingdom wasn't always this way. A generation ago the kingdom was in ruins. Its buildings were mere shacks, its noble customs were dishonored, and its people were in disarray. The land stayed that way for ages . . .

. . . until a great king arose and led this land into its great and golden age. This age of peace lasted so long that nearly no one had remembered how bad things used to be.

But soon came the day that the king was to retire and pass on his throne to his son, prince Juna. Juna was a near perfect candidate for the next king. He was athletic, very handsome, and a pleasant person to be around. Nearly everyone who met Juna immediately began to like him.

Alas, came the day when the king announced that in a year's time he would finally pass on the throne to his son.

. . . but this decision made a lot of people uncomfortable, for Juna had one crucial flaw: Juna wasn't very wise.

It was not that the prince was unintelligent, but rather that he made bad decisions. On nearly any and every occasion when Juna was given responsibility over something, he would squander it.

If you gave him money he would spend it unwisely.

If you gave him a crucial task he would fail at it.

But, scariest of all, if you gave him command over people disaster was bound to soon follow.

Despite his talents and achievements, the prince had always worried about his one flaw. In the back of his mind he feared that this one flaw would derail his reign as king.

A few days after the announcement, Juna was walking through the marketplace when he overheard some people talking. Hearing his name, he hid behind a corner and listened to the peoples' conversation. He peeked from around the corner so that they would not see him. Their words confirmed his worst fears. As much as they liked him, the people were nervous that the prince would lead to the kingdom's downfall.

"Did you hear that the prince is going to become king next year?" said a merchant.

"Why yes I did, and I fear for the worst my friend I'm afraid," said a lady buying wheat.

"Why is that?" asked someone else in the crowd. "The prince looks like a strapping young lad. A mere chip off the old block I'd say."

"But that's the problem," another person spoke. "He's got the stature of a mountain, but the brains of a pebble!"

"What a terrible thing to say!" said another woman.

Another man stepped into the crowd. "But he's right I tell you! My son was in the learning academy with him and he says it's true! The prince has got the book smarts my son says, but when you give the boy something to do he bumbles it all up. Mark my words my friends, when the crown is passed to that young lad you can expect the dark days to be returning swiftly."

There were a couple gasps and some hushed murmuring after these last words. The worst thing however, was the look of concern that grew on several peoples' faces. Some looked conflicted, while others seemed to buy the notion fully; however, despite how reluctant they may or may not have been to believe it, they all seemed to agree in one way or another.

After hearing this conversation in the marketplace, Juna's heart sunk in his chest. In his mind Juna saw all the possible disasters that could happen under his leadership. He worried that his foolishness would lead to the kingdom's ruin. With each passing thought, his fears and doubts began to overwhelm him.

He ran away from the marketplace in a panic. He had to stop his father from passing down the throne to him. When he arrived, his father was sitting calmly in the bed chambers, reading over a scroll and sipping some hot tea.

Juna ran up to him and expressed his fears. "Oh, Father! Please do not pass the throne down to me. I am not ready for such a responsibility. Please I beg of you pass down this mantle to someone worthier than I."

Throughout his plea the king listened calmly. He took another sip of his tea and bid the prince to sit in a chair.

"Calm yourself and breathe," said the king.

The prince did so, but still felt sick to his stomach.

"Now tell me my son, why do you wish to give away what is rightfully yours?"

"It's the announcement father. Do you hear what the people are saying?" he exclaimed. "They're saying I may bring the kingdom down when you retire. Some are saying that I am foolish and will thus be a foolish king. They talk of the dark days returning again because of my folly."

"Do you think yourself a fool my son?" asked the king, raising an eyebrow.

The prince shrugged. "I don't know what to think father, for I have many conflicting feelings in my heart. On one hand I feel that I am very capable, for I have trained for this role all my life. Nevertheless, I cannot ignore my many failures and farces thus far! I have squandered so many opportunities and made so many foolish choices in the past. How can I not thus think that I will be no different in a year's time?"

The king curled his beard in his fingers, looking solemn and composed all the while. He pursed his lips and scrunched his eyebrows as if to think. "Hmm I see . . . " he muttered. "And you think I should thus pass the crown onto someone else you say?"

The prince nodded his head.

The king's resolute look remained for a few moments. The prince could tell his father was thinking deeply about it. His heart skipped a few beats as he anticipated what his father would say.

The king nodded his head, but very slightly. Juna even wasn't sure it was a nod at all. In fact, the king looked not as if he were nodding to the prince, but rather to himself.

Finally, the prince's anxiousness got the better of him and he asked. "So, what do you say Father? Will you pass the crown onto someone else?"

The king said nothing for another moment. Then he spoke, "My son, I have some things to tell you. Some of which you may like . . . and some of which you may not. Firstly, no, I will not give the crown and its duties to another suitor. You are the rightful heir and the burden of it is yours whether you feel ready for it or not."

The prince's heart sunk again. Juna began to put his face in his hands but was stopped by his father's upturned fingers. The prince looked up to see his father with a proud smile upon him. He was holding one finger up with his other hand, as if to halt him from what he was doing.

He continued softly. "I understand your concern, my son. In fact, your concern shows that you are a very considerate and thoughtful young man. But I will not pass this mantle onto anyone else because you are, in fact, very capable for the job. I have watched you, my son, and I can honestly tell you that you are very talented. You've excelled in combat and navigation, you're exceedingly compassionate and driven, and are more intelligent than you give yourself credit for. All of these are necessary qualities of a great king. You see, I know of your past failures and I know, in fact, what has been the crucial cause for them all.

"And it is not your lack of intellect, but rather your lack of *wisdom*."

The prince looked confused. "But Father I don't understand. You just said that I was very smart. How can I be intelligent and lack wisdom?"

The king took another sip of his tea. When he finished he chuckled and said, "My son, being cunning or intelligent is not the same as being *wise*. Why, many of your forefathers were a great deal more intelligent than I, but none of them possessed the essential wisdom needed to become a great king."

"So how did you become so wise?" the prince asked.

"Well through several things: a great amount of time passed, mistakes made and learned from, a few key victories attained, and several embarrassing defeats but most of all, I found a great teacher to teach me. And that my son is what I'm going to advise for you, a great teacher."

Juna's face lit up. "Oh, thank you, Father!" he shouted. "I will not take this lightly. When do we begin?"

The king took another sip of tea. "It's good that you are so eager, for you will need it, but I will not be your instructor. There is one who is far better suited to teach you than I. I recommend that you should go to him and see what he can teach you of wisdom."

The prince's face drooped a little, for he was excited about learning from his father. He took a deep breath and asked, "Well then, who will teach me? What's his name?"

"The teacher's name is Hokmah the wise. You will find him beyond the eastern forests of Bilgelik. He's quite a peculiar fellow and he works in some rather mysterious ways, but I am sure that his teachings will change your life forever."

The prince patted his thighs and stood up. "Well then it's settled, to the forests of Bilgelik I will go."

The king nodded. "Indeed. As I've said before I will not give the throne to anyone else, but you. Nevertheless, I will continue to wait for a year until you return. When you come back all will go as I've just said, I will step down and you will become king. However, before you go I must advise you on a few things.

"Firstly, the forests of Bilgelik are very far away and can be a very foreboding place, so pack well and be wary of its landscapes and wildlife." The king stood and stepped out of the room. In a few moments he returned with a scroll and a quill. "Secondly, I would advise you to take this scroll. Hokmah will insist you write down his teachings and *meditate on them day and night,* so be sure not to lose it."

The prince took the scroll and quill into his hands. "I won't Father, I promise."

The king smiled. "And my last word of advice is the most important advice I can give you on the path of becoming wiser. As you travel, no matter how busy or stressed you are, always be sure to *treat others like you would yourself.* Overall, I think you will do well my son. Rest tonight and worry not. Eat plenty and pack well. You will leave at the crack of dawn tomorrow and thus you will be on your way to becoming what you were always meant to be."

The prince hugged his father. They bowed to one another and the prince took off to do as his father had told him.

Juna woke the next morning and put on his traveling gear. His father met him outside of his bed chambers. The king guided Juna toward the outskirts of their land where they said their goodbyes to each other.

So, with scroll in hand, Juna began his trek toward the lauded home of Hokmah the wise.

It took several weeks, and the road was long and winding, but Juna was persistent and endured it all. Finally, he came upon the mark in the map that was supposed to be the home of Hokmah, but when he looked around he saw nothing but woods.

"I must've read the map wrong," said Juna. "Surely the great Hokmah could not live here."

Juna was beginning to change course when he heard a squeaky voice.

"Psst, psst. Mister traveler, sir?" said the voice, but when Juna turned around he saw no one. "Psst, down here please, sir," said the voice again.

The prince looked down to see what was speaking to him. Juna had a hard time spotting the thing since nearly half of its body was concealed by a small rock. It looked like a small lizard or snake, but its body seemed considerably pale and blotched. Whatever it was, it wasn't doing so well.

"Psst, excuse me sir, I hate to disturb you, but could I ask you a favor?" asked the creature.

Juna jumped a little. He had never heard of a talking lizard. Stuttering he blurted out, "Ah, yes! What do you need, Mr. Lizard?"

"Oh, thank you good sir," it replied quaintly. "You see, I'm a newt, and I have found myself getting too far away from my pond in search of food. Well, I found the food all right, but I've gotten myself caught under this rock. It's the heaviest thing! However, my biggest concern is that if I stay away from the pond too much longer I fear I may dry up. I hate to ask but could you be a dear and lift this thing off of me?"

"Why, sure, Mr. Newt," Juna replied.

Juna picked up the rock and threw it into the woods.

The newt rejoiced. "Good heavens, thank you! Why, I thought I would never get out from under that thing! Thanks, so much Mr. . . . ."

"It's Prince Juna of the kingdom of Eskolar. And you're very welcome. I hope you find your pond, sir," said Juna. He smiled, bowed, and began changing his course.

Or . . . at least he tried to.

Before the prince could leave the newt spoke again. "Oh, excuse me, Prince. I hate to ask, but could I request another favor before you go?"

The prince was a little annoyed. He couldn't spare much time. Nevertheless, remembering his father's words, he forced a smile and turned around.

"Why . . . yes, Mr. Newt," Juna said.

"I do hate to be such a nuisance, especially to royalty like yourself, but I don't have much strength in me, and I fear I won't be able to get to the pond by myself. Could you take me there?"

"How far is it?" asked the prince.

"Oh, not far," said the newt. "It's just a few of your human footsteps beyond those trees there."

The prince sighed under his breath and reluctantly agreed. He gently picked up the shriveled newt and began to walk through the woods.

So, they walked.

. . . and walked . . .

. . . and walked some more.

After an hour or so had passed the prince became very frustrated, for this newt must surely be taking advantage of his kindness.

Finally, the two ended up at the pond. He gently laid the newt in a shallow puddle. The water had an instant effect. At once the newt's skin went from a blotched beige to a brilliant chrome.

"Good heavens! What a relief! Thanks, my friend," said the newt, his voice now clear and crisp.

Juna nodded and said. "You're very welcome!" He was glad the ordeal was over. "Have a great day." He quickly turned to leave, but the newt spoke again before he could depart.

"Oh, but Prince Juna, you mustn't leave before I'm allowed to give you something in return, for surely it would be wrong not to give as I've received."

The prince tried to decline, but the newt was insistent. Juna gave in and allowed the newt to try and help him, though he was unsure how on earth a newt could help him.

"Before you helped me did I hear you mention something about the great Hokmah the wise?"

The prince's eyes perked. "Why yes! I'm looking to learn from him so that I may become wise enough to be a great king."

The newt smiled. "Well, my boy you're in luck! I not only know where Hokmah resides, but the two of us are great friends! Since you helped me when I was in need, I will guide you to Hokmah's abode."

Juna's eyes lit up with excitement. "Thanks so much!" he shouted. He picked up the newt and scooped some pond water into his pail. He didn't intend on coming all the way back to the pond again.

So, the prince and the newt made their way through more woods, until they came across an abandoned shack on the outskirts of the forest.

"And here we are!" the newt exclaimed.

Juna was immediately confused. He saw nothing he'd expect from such an esteemed wise man. Nevertheless, he walked to the door of the shack. A piece of parchment was hung on it. It read:

To all prospective students, seekers, or otherwise;

I am away at the moment. The time of my return may vary. Feel free to any and all of my belongings while I am away, including even my bed.

If you are in a hurry to learn please carry on but waiting would be wise.

Sincerely,

Hokmah

Juna's hopes fell. He had come all this way, just for Hokmah to be away from home. *Perhaps he has just walked to town and will be back in a few hours,* Juna thought. He could surely wait that long.

And so, the prince waited . . .

. . . and waited . . .

. . . and waited . . .

Until night finally fell. Frustrated, the prince made camp outside the shack.

But the very next day Hokmah was still nowhere to be found. *Perhaps,* he thought, *he must be walking back from another city.* Maybe he won't be back for a few days or so. Surely, he could wait that long.

And again, the prince and the newt waited for the wise man.

So, they waited a day . . .

. . . and another day . . .

. . . and another, until finally Juna became frustrated once more.

How long would he have to wait?

He read the note again, turning it over, and reading it over and over to see if he could find a clue as to how much longer he'd have to wait. Alas, he did not find any other notes or clues. Deflated, the prince sat down on a stump and pondered.

It's been nearly a week. At this point he has to be very far away, thought the prince. His frustration mounting, he began pondering aloud. "How long has he been gone anyway? If he had left very recently than it may be a month or so before he'll return. If it's going to take that long before I even start perhaps I need to find another way of gaining wisdom."

But before he acted on those thoughts, the last sentence in the note kept recurring to him.

If you are in a hurry to learn please carry on but waiting would be wise.

He thought hard about that sentence. His mind mulled it over like a dog chewing a tough piece of meat.

Finally, it clicked.

"Wise! To wait would be wise!" he exclaimed. "It must be a riddle or some kind of test. It's a test of patience!"

With that thought he resolved within himself that no matter how long it took he would wait.

As if reading his mind, the newt spoke up. "Well, if we're going to be here for a while you might as well go inside the shack and see what he has. After all he did invite you to use it."

The prince agreed.

He opened the door to the rickety shack. Inside there was only a small cot, a shovel, a few gardening tools, some fishing gear, and a small canoe. He felt a little bad about using someone else's bed to sleep in, but it would be better than sleeping outside again. More confusing still, the prince could not figure out why the only other things inside were a shovel and some fishing tools. There was no evidence of a garden outside and the only source of water was very far away.

The newt climbed out of the pail, crawled onto the shovel, and turned to the prince. "I have an idea that might give us something to do while we wait."

"What is it?" Juna asked.

"Well, as you know, the water in the pail is beginning to dry up. Since we are going to be here a while it would be a good help to both of us if we could keep some water around so that we don't have to keep going back and forth to the pond."

The prince definitely agreed about the last part. He nodded and the newt continued on.

"Well since we have a shovel here we could dig a little hole to store water in. You could dig one hole for drinking water and another for myself to swim in."

The prince nodded. He wasn't very excited about building a swimming pool for a newt, but it would at least give him something to do.

Juna took the shovel and began to dig two holes. It was hard work, but also satisfying in a way. The only thing that truly bothered him was the newt's insistence on digging such a big hole. One time during the digging Juna had stopped, thinking he was finished. The newt examined the pools then went back to crawl on his shoulder.

With a quizzical look upon him the newt said, "Hmm, I think we'll need some bigger holes don't you think?"

"I don't see why. They're pretty deep," replied Juna.

"Well that's true, but you don't want all your water to dry up because the hole is too small. Besides, as you may have noticed, I've grown while we've been here."

Juna took a look at the newt. He was right. The newt had grown to nearly twice his size in the span of a few days. By now he was certainly the biggest newt he'd ever seen. Juna was tired, but Hokmah was still not here. Besides, what else was there to do?

So, he dug all day and even into some part of the night.

The next day, Juna, muscles sore from the previous day's work, awoke thinking that it was indeed time to call it quits on the digging. But when he looked at the newt again, somehow, he'd grown even larger. He was now nearly as long as Juna's leg. Knowing the newt would insist on a bigger hole. He dug some more, until finally the two holes were deeper than he was tall.

Panting, the prince muttered, "If he grows any more I'll just cut off his tail and be done with it."

The newt walked over to the hole. Juna held his breath. Fortunately, the newt, if you could still call him a newt, nodded as if to say, "This'll do."

"Yes! Now it's time to fill it up," Juna said with relief. "Let's head back to the pond."

The newt scratched his chin with his now very long tail. "Hmm, I've been thinking, Your Highness, about that. If you're going to be drinking from this water and I'm going to be living in it, we mustn't use something as dirty as pond water."

This irritated the prince, for certainly the newt had no problems with pond water before. Nevertheless, he swallowed his frustration.

The prince let out a reluctant breath. "Well, what do you propose?"

"I know of a river not far from here. It feeds the pond where I was living in. Word round the forest calls it the River of Living Water. While the pond water is murky, creatures say that the river water is always clear and fresh. If we head a little ways up the brook, we'll find the river and get ourselves some good water."

The prince thought about it then nodded. "Okay. Let's look for the river."

Knowing the newt's sense of direction, he readied himself for another long trek.

The two trekked to the river, the oversized newt leading the way. The river was more beautiful than Juna had expected. The water looked clear, smelled fresh, and it almost seemed to sparkle. It was one of the most beautiful things he'd ever witnessed. He dipped his hand in and took a sip. It was tasty to drink. In fact, the living water seemed to nourish him more than the finest meals from the palace. The prince drank until he couldn't drink anymore while the newt dove in and out of the water like a lizard shaped dolphin. Finally, once they were satisfied, Juna filled up the buckets and ran back to the hut.

It took several trips to fill up the holes, but the living water gave him enough energy for the job.

When at last the pools were finished Juna and the newt rejoiced. Juna could bathe and drink from the tasty water at any time he wished. Meanwhile the newt continued to bask in his newfound swimming hole. In fact, the newt barely seemed to leave the water, even when it was time for dinner.

The next morning Juna awoke to yet another surprise from his friend. The newt grew again, but this time he began resembling something like a large carnivorous lizard. His snout had turned from round to narrow. The pads that were his feet had become claws. He'd grown stubby teeth and his tender skin had hardened into sparkling scales.

The newt had come out of the water and was now lying on a rock. Juna walked over to him to find his face contorted as if he were sad.

"Hi, Mr. Newt. What's wrong?" asked Juna.

Despite looking fiercer the newt was still just as cordial. "Well it's nothing serious I suppose, but it's just that I'm very hungry. You see, I've been eating my usual diet of insects and grubs the entire morning, but it seems I just cannot get full. Now I haven't the foggiest idea what to do."

Juna looked along the newt's long frame. The problem was obvious.

"Well, Mr. Newt. I don't think that's too much of a surprise. I mean look at you. You're quite a big fellow now. I don't think all the bugs in the world would keep you full."

The newt's face drooped. "Oh bother, I'm afraid you're right, Your Highness, but whatever am I to do?"

The prince felt bad for his friend. He thought hard about food. While the newt's usual diet could not sustain him, the prince had no worries about food. He had packed a lot of food with him when he had left. Even when that ran out he could always hunt for some more. But what could he hunt for a giant newt?

He glanced at the pool and an idea immediately sprang into his head.

He turned to the newt and snapped his fingers. "The fishing rod!" Juna said. "How about I grab you some fish?"

The newt blinked. "If you think that will help, surely I'll indeed try."

Juna ran inside the hut and grabbed the fishing gear and the buckets. Then he headed back toward the river. He used the rod to fish in the deeper parts of the river. In the shallow banks he caught some fish with his spear and shot some more with his bow. Thinking for both himself and the newt he decided to bring back as much as possible. At last, when he could carry no more, the prince made his way back to the shack.

When he met up with the newt he reached in the bucket and brought out a hefty sized fish. For a moment the newt seemed puzzled. He sniffed the fish and looked at it curiously. At that moment the prince recognized the irony in this situation. He knew that fish often ate newts and salamanders, and now he was trying to get a newt to eat a fish. *It must be strange trying to eat what usually eats you,* the prince thought. He imagined a lion with an apple in its mouth like a pork dinner. The thought made him laugh, and as the moments passed he began realizing that maybe this was a bad idea.

However, just as he was about to put the fish back, a ferocious instinct overtook the newt and he swallowed the fish. After the first fish the newt became insatiable.

"Good heavens! That is good! Thanks, Your Highness!" exclaimed the newt. "Please tell me you have more!"

The prince smiled and took out another fish. In a matter of seconds, the fish was snapped up and gobbled down. Afraid for his own hand now, the prince threw the fish into the newt's pool. In a flash the newt jumped in and began wolfing the fish down.

Juna was so excited to see the newt's enjoyment, he came up with the idea to bring back some live fish, so the newt could have them whenever he needed. It would be as if he had his own pond. He shared the idea with the newt.

"Why that would be a splendid idea, my boy!" the newt exclaimed. "If we're going to create our own little pond then we'll need to expand the pool a little more."

The prince became very excited about their little project. The difficulty of creating it was trumped by their enthusiasm.

"Indeed. You're right, Mr. Newt. I'll get started on that tomorrow. Then we'll put the fish in." Juna scratched his chin.

"And I'll help you my lad, for indeed you've done much for me," said the newt. He looked at his claws and flexed them. "I tell you what, lad, come the morrow just take care of getting the fish and I'll do the digging. It seems I have the proper equipment for digging now anyways."

The two laughed, ate some more fish, and went to bed.

The next morning Juna awoke at the crack of dawn and prepared his equipment. This time he filled his buckets up with water to put the fish into, gathered his gear, and proceeded back to the river. The fish were harder to come by this day. It took him most of the day to catch half the amount he had before. Nevertheless, he headed back to the shack with his haul.

It won't matter much anyways, thought the prince. *Our personal pond won't be ready for a few days at the least anyhow.*

To his surprise, he returned to find that the newt's pool had doubled in size.

Juna went to the edge of the pool and gawked at it. The bottom of the pond was draped with little plants and roots, as a lake would have been. There were already birds and small animals that had stopped by to drink from the water. Meanwhile, at the other edge of the pond was the newt digging away.

The newt spoke as he was digging. "Back from the first haul I see! Just lay the fish in. They'll adjust to the pool pretty soon."

The prince was amazed at the newt's progress. *The newt would make a great construction worker,* Juna thought.

"He'd make a fortune at the rate he works," he muttered to himself. The two feasted on only a few of the fish then said goodnight.

The next day the prince proceeded back to the river. However, this day the fish were even harder to catch. The small fish in the shallows were nowhere to be found and with each cast bigger and bigger fish caught the bait. They fought against Juna harder and harder with each cast. Juna was baffled that fishing had become so hard. He never had to struggle when it came to fishing. Nevertheless, as the hours waned, it took more and more effort to bring in a single one. He returned with a paltry amount compared to the previous days. Juna found that the newt had doubled the size of the pool again.

As with the hole digging and water filling, their little project took an incredible effort to finish. Since the pool was bigger he'd first have to bring in more water to fill it. The bigger the pool the more fish it would require. Making matters worse the fish seemed harder and harder to catch.

The prince wanted to call it quits on their project several times, but Hokmah still hadn't returned. So Juna would think to himself, *Since I've promised myself I'd stay, what else is there to do?*

He made another resolution to finish the project, despite how hard it had become.

In the proceeding days Juna and the newt became lost in their work.

After a while their idea started to take shape. Sometimes a heavy rainstorm would come and fill up the lake for them. Juna grew stronger and better at bringing in the bigger fish. Even some of the fish in the pool had begun to multiply. Before they knew it, ospreys and eagles visited the pool to hunt for fish. The sight of sea hawks assured them that they were making good progress.

Finally, the prince tried fishing from their pond to get their food. The pond was so big now, they started calling it "the lake." The prince looked out onto the lake's surface to see wafts of insects gobbled up by fish.

To confirm that they had enough fish Juna sent the newt into the water to see the state of their lake.

In a few moments the newt emerged and told the prince, "Well my boy, it seems at last we've crammed that lake chock full of fish! Why I could barely swim without bumping into one of them. Let us feast tonight and celebrate!"

The two roasted, boiled, and fried as many fish as they could consume. They told each other stories from their lives back at home and had a merry time.

During their feast, the newt came up with yet another suggestion. He wolfed down another fish and licked his claws clean of any trace of his meal.

Between licks he said. "Good heavens, Your Highness, I've never had such a feast!" With a jolt of excitement, the newt stopped licking and shouted, "Hey, do you know what this needs?"

"What?" asked the prince, between bites of fish himself.

"It needs some variety!" exclaimed the newt. "Yes indeed! Tomorrow we could gather some crayfish and crab, and even some grubs to go with it!"

The prince raised an eyebrow and thought about it. Since they had food at their demand, perhaps they now could think of adding other things to their diet. He had become so used to eating just fish that he'd forgotten that in the palace he'd always had an array of different foods to eat.

"You know," said Juna, "that's actually a good idea. How about we do that tomorrow morning? I'll leave the bugs to you though."

They laughed, finished their meal, and went to bed.

The next morning, they went back to the river and searched for other foods. It didn't take them long. In the shallows the prince found crayfish and crab for himself, while the newt found frogs and snails for himself. From the neighboring trees they found nuts and berries that they hadn't noticed before.

Perhaps we could plant a tree from them, or maybe even a garden, thought the prince.

The two used the same method for their new prey as they had for the fish. They were content to eat very little of the new items until they grew in abundance. Meanwhile the prince planted a few of the seeds and nuts.

In time bushes of berries and little tree stalks began to sprout. The crabs, snails, frogs, and other newfound creatures became usual sights amongst their lake. When they felt it was right they gathered the new prey, the fish, and a few of the berries then proceeded to make another feast.

Their idea worked well.

"Great heavens above! This is fantastic!" roared the newt, licking his claws. "Now what did I tell you, my lad. See what a little variety can do for a palate!"

The prince smiled and nodded. Indeed, the newt was right. The many different tastes reminded him of his meals in the palace. Though he didn't know for how much longer he'd have to stay, he began to think of this little area as a home away from home.

The next morning the prince awoke to a scary surprise. When he walked outside he was shocked to see a wolf nearby, scouring the remnants of the food from the night before. The wolf turned and snarled at him. Juna was frightened. He'd left his bow and spear in the shack.

The wolf lunged for him, and Juna fell backwards. But just in the nick of time the newt burst out of the water and flared his teeth and claws. By this time the newt was even bigger than Juna, and it frightened the wolf.

The newt sheathed his claws and turned to Juna as the wolf fled. "Are you alright, Your Highness?" asked the newt.

"Yes, thanks to you!" said the prince. "Good heavens that was frightening! I haven't seen a wolf this entire time. It just shocked me that is all."

The newt nodded and turned to look at their surroundings. Juna followed his gaze. Slowly they both started to notice their surroundings. The ground was littered with fish bones, crab shells, and half eaten berries.

"No wonder the wolf came," Juna said. "It seems we've been a bit careless after our feast."

The newt nudged the prince and turned toward the lake. "That's not the only thing we've left unattended your highness."

The prince turned and looked at the lake. The lake's once clear water was murky and dirty. Animal dung was on the forest floor and weeds were growing in their garden.

The prince took a deep breath, sighed, but then stood up. "Well it seems today we've got some cleaning to do."

"Indeed, my boy," said the newt.

The two began cleaning the area. The work was long, tedious, and boring. They gathered the fish bones, nutshells, and dung then ground it into fertilizer for the garden. The prince uprooted the weeds in the garden while the newt searched for the remaining predators and scared them away.

To clean the lake, they took the small canoe out from the shed and went out into the water. They took the buckets and scooped out whatever filth they could find in the lake. When the water became low Juna made trips to the river to bring back some fresh water.

After a few days day the lake was finally looking sparkling and beautiful again.

Nevertheless, as happy as they were to get the lake looking new again, the work had taken its toll.

After emptying a bucket of fresh water, Juna sat back on the stump, exhausted from their work.

The newt walked up to him and looked at him curiously. He scratched a claw along his long chin as if thinking over something. The prince looked up and raised an eyebrow.

"I know what that look means," said the prince, weakly. "What do we have to do now?"

"Well, to be honest, I'm thinking of just the opposite. You know the two of us have been at this for a while, and I think we deserve a little respite." At last he straightened out his claw and smiled. "I know! How about we have a little fun!"

The prince raised an eyebrow, at last the newt came up with an idea that he totally agreed with. "I'm up for that, but what do you have in mind?" asked Juna.

The corner of the newt's mouth raised in a mischievous smile. "Well how about we take a little boat ride down the river? That ought to be fun. We can fish and relax as we roll down the river."

The idea sounded nice to Juna. "You know what, that sounds pretty good."

So, the next morning they packed their gear and made their way back out to the river. They took their time and fished for a few hours, enjoying the time away from their work.

But then something unfortunate happened.

Juna was fishing when the newt shouted, "Juna hurry! Turn and look!"

The prince was startled. He turned and looked to find that his backpack was rolling down the river. It was already too far to reach out and grab, but he couldn't let the pack get away from him. It had everything of his in it, including the scroll his father said not to lose. The prince scrambled for the canoe and rushed into the water. The newt jumped in right after and they shoved off to catch up to the pack.

They were gaining on the pack when the wind suddenly turned wild. Like a startled nest of hornets, the cool morning air had turned into a raging tempest. Water lapped in and around the boat. Their canoe bounced and rocked along the water.

The pack dropped in and out of their sight as it bounced amidst the raging water, but the prince couldn't let the pack get away.

The winds blew for a long time. For hours the two rocked along the winding river desperately keeping their eyes peeled for the pack. Despite their best efforts though, they lost sight of it. The prince paddled and paddled, but it was no use. The river's surface was so choppy he wouldn't have been able to see it even if it were right next to him.

The prince sat back deflated. He didn't want to give up on the hunt, but he finally had no choice. There was nothing he could do.

Defeated, Juna pulled his garments over his head to shield him from the rain. Luckily for the newt, the water seemed to roll off his scaly skin. He crawled over to the prince and wrapped his tail around Juna, shielding him further from the rampaging wind. Focusing on their survival, they held on to the boat for dear life as the wind lashed the rushing water.

It grew dark in the waning hours. They had said nothing for a long time. The sounds of the rushing water and swirling winds lulled and calmed them. They were nearly asleep when the prince noticed that one sound had disappeared.

"The wind," he muttered. "Mr. Newt do you notice? The wind is gone."

The newt raised his head and rotated it. "Alas, you're right, Your Highness. The air is as still as ever."

At last the water's surface became flat and calm. With the river so still and tranquil the prince saw things in the water that he hadn't noticed before. Fish of all kinds were swimming along the current. Some fish swam right next to the canoe as if it weren't even there. There were little lizards and frogs that skimmed along the banks. Fireflies illuminated the air while dragonflies and a host of other insects bobbed along the surface. The more he looked, the more he noticed about the river and all that made it what it was.

An idea came back to him. Since the water was still now perhaps he could see the pack.

"I bet I can find my pack now, if it's not too far away that is," said the prince.

"Indeed. Why don't you give it a shot?" the newt said.

The prince looked around, taking his time to scan each portion of the river.

He surveyed every inch of water he could see. After a few anxious moments he finally found the pack. Of all places, the bag was bobbing just in front of the canoe. Juna reached and grabbed the pack, thankful that the debacle was over with.

In an unfamiliarly dark tone, the newt said, "Hmm. This doesn't bode well."

"What do you mean?" asked the prince.

"It's pretty dark now and, it seems this river is a bit bigger than we've thought."

"How do you know that?"

"Well, have you noticed that we can't spot the banks anymore?" asked the newt.

Juna turned and looked around. It was hard to tell through the darkness, but the edges of the river were indeed nowhere to found. He looked back and around, but it all looked the same. There was only water for miles to see. He didn't even know rivers could get this big.

With the same foreboding tone, the newt scratched his chin and said, "Good heavens, I believe we're in the very heart of the river now."

"What does that mean?" asked the prince.

The newt was about to speak when the boat jolted violently. In an instant the newt was tossed from the boat and into the river.

"Mr. Newt!" shouted the prince.

He heard a splash nearby, but the newt was nowhere to be found. The prince began slowing the boat when a deep humming sound began rumbling through the canoe. The prince's heart stopped. The water below him seemed to darken even more, but in the shape of a long menacing line. The humming started again, but this time even louder. The dead of night was coming fast and in a matter of moments the only light that could be seen was moonlight. The crickets had stopped chirping and an eerie silence had overtaken the river.

A deep rumble rolled through the canoe again. Then, as if a large tree had risen from its bottom, a dark figure slowly emerged from the river. Though the object or creature was extremely large, it was too dark outside to see any of its features. The only thing the prince could make out was a large white circle that was the unmistakable sight of an eyeball.

The prince froze where he was and tried averting his eyes but found that he couldn't. The sight of this creature was too amazing and terrifying to look away. To his horror the rumble began again, and he felt the creature's hot breath roll over the canoe.

Juna slowly reached back for his paddle, but, as if knowing what he was doing, the creature reacted. It let out a short guttural growl and opened its maw. Its mouth was a long as the canoe. The prince paddled forward frantically. He cruised through the water at top speed, but the creature was faster.

The creature's glowing eye emerged beside the canoe. Juna shouted and turned the boat just before it opened its gigantic mouth and snapped at him. He tried moving forward again, but this time even harder. Even as he tried the creature gained on him. The creature's head slammed against the back of the canoe and caused it to swirl in the water. The prince bumped his head against the boat but held on as tight as he could. The creature roared a mighty and terrifying roar. Its roar sounded like a thousand cracks of thunder and the roar of a hundred lions.

Juna was terrified, but for some reason, something the newt said occurred to him at that moment.

"I'd say we're at the very heart of river now," the newt had said.

But why would that matter now? he thought. *Where I am doesn't mean anything with this beast after me!*

But then it hit him. He recalled earlier what they had said about the banks.

If I can just make it to the bank, maybe I can I can get away, he thought.

The prince rowed for where he thought was left. He just hoped he could get there in time.

The creature's attack however became even more intense. Its roar was louder and more terrible than anything the prince had ever heard in his young life. Quicker than the blink of an eye, the creature lunged for the prince and something along the creature's body scraped him.

Juna was in pain but gathered his senses and paddled onward. The creature lunged again but missed. He could feel the cool night air and the creature's hot breath crash over him like a wave. It roared again and snapped its maw just behind him. The only thing the prince could think of was to paddle and paddle . . .

. . . and paddle.

. . . until the finally he began to note the creature's roaring had died down.

He didn't dare stop. At last he caught a glimpse of the bank in the distance and sped toward it. To his delight the creature seemed to finally leave him alone. Or at least that's what he'd hoped for.

He crashed onto the bank and jumped out of the boat. He fell onto the mud and heaved in and out, desperately trying to calm himself. After a few moments he finally stood up, but when he turned around he found a terrifying sight. Behind the boat, not more than ten feet away, was the beast, or rather . . .

. . . its head.

It was still underwater, but the creature was looking at him through that large white eye. The prince did not move for surely the creature was contemplating whether or not it could still reach him from that distance. Knowing roughly of the creature's size, he didn't doubt that it could.

But then a surprising thing happened. There was a humming sound again, but this time it was lighter and less menacing. It was still perhaps a growl of some kind, but he couldn't shake the feeling that the creature had a different intention than before. The humming continued and as it did it started to turn into a sort of whimper or moan. It faintly resembled something like the singing of birds or the strumming of a harp.

Then the creature suddenly brightened like a bright silver torch. The light nearly had the same effect as the darkness. The creature's luminescence was so bright it nearly hurt his eyes. Too bright to stare at, the prince still could not make out what the creature was. Though it was intense, the creature's light somehow began to soothe him. It was as if the creature was now pleased with him. A few moments ago, this creature was trying to devour him. Nevertheless, the longer he stared and the more he listened, the surer he was that this creature was now showing him some sign of benevolence or thanks. Perhaps this was the creature saying that it was pleased that the prince had left his territory.

The illumination continued for a few more moments before it dimmed, and the creature slowly receded back into the water. The prince's heart was pounding, but this time there was not only fear, but also wonder. He was surely frightened by the whole ordeal on this river, but something about what had just occurred made him feel better somehow.

The good feeling lasted only for a few minutes before a lurking sense of dread came over him.

It was about the loss of his friend Mr. Newt. Though the beast didn't capture him, it must've surely caught the newt when he was tossed into the water. He had grown to be great friends with the newt and it was a terrible feeling to lose him as he had.

Saddened, the prince gathered his pack and the canoe then made his way into the woods to make camp.

He awoke the next morning in a foul mood. His body sore, his clothes still damp, and still mourning the loss of his best friend, Juna slowly and silently packed his gear for the long trek back to the shack. He wouldn't be using the river anytime soon. During the midst of his hike back he heard a shuffling in the leaves behind him. At first, he merely shrugged it off.

It must be some sort of squirrel or bird, he thought.

He walked again, but a few moments later, the shuffling continued. This same pattern happened for a few yards.

Something was following him.

Juna slowly took his bow in hand and notched an arrow. He was in no mood for any other surprise attacks; whatever creature was lurking behind him this time was going to be in for a fight. He took another step and turned around.

His mouth fell open with surprise.

Behind him, covered in mud was the newt.

The newt's eyes went wide, "Good heavens, Your Highness!" stammered the newt. "I'd hoped we were on better terms than an armed greeting."

The prince could not believe it. He was so happy he dropped his bow and threw his arms around Newt.

"By all the kings of Eskolar!" exclaimed Juna, "I'm so happy to see you! Tell me how on earth did you survive?"

"Well, it's a rather shameful story if I do admit, sire," the newt said.

"How do you mean?" replied the prince.

"Well if you recall, I was mentioning how we'd best find the shore when I was tossed from the boat."

The prince nodded.

"I was already surprised to find myself in the water, but then, as you no doubt found out, there was that awful creature in the water. Well, I hate to admit it sir, but when I gathered the sight of that beast I could think only of saving myself. I'm ashamed to say that I swam away and hid myself on the bottom of the river. I should have come back for you, to warn you, help you or something, but I didn't. I know there's no apologizing for it, but can you find it in your heart to forgive me?"

The prince was flabbergasted. He was so happy to see his friend that he couldn't possibly be angry with him.

"Why, of course, Mr. Newt! In fact, I don't think there's anything to forgive. When that creature attacked I did all I could to get to safety and didn't go back for you. I'm as much to blame as you are. As far as I'm concerned there's no apologies needed. I'm just happy you're alive."

The newt smiled a toothy grin. "Why thank you, lad, you're indeed royalty my good friend. Now let's shove off back to the shack."

The prince nodded, and the two set off for the shack. As it turned out, they had indeed traveled a long way down the river. It took them nearly the entire day to make it back. As they traveled, an unsettling change of weather was setting in. That morning had started out sunny and beautiful, but by midafternoon the skies were clad with silver clouds. There soon was a whistle in the air. It flowed through the trees and increased in pitch as they got closer.

"It looks as if the weather's getting bad," said the newt. "We'd better get back as fast as we can."

And so, the two trotted through the woods.

The newt's prediction was right. As they marched, the weather worsened. The prince looked up to the sky and saw the silver patch of clouds had turned into a pitch-black mass. A humming noise began to rumble through the air. It was as if yesterday's events on the river had come back, though the prince knew it was no beast that was roaring now. What roared now was the biggest and most terrible storm he would ever come to know.

Just as he looked up, there was a blinding flash and a loud crack behind him. It was lightning! The lightning bolt had struck a large tree behind him.

"Run!" shouted the newt, his voice deafened by the roaring thunder.

Then, like fire from the bellows of a dragon, monstrous winds suddenly came forth. They nearly knocked Juna off his feet as they came rushing through the forest.

Juna dropped the canoe and the two ran through the forest. The prince had never known such fright. Innumerous bolts of lightning fell from the heavens, shattering trees and scarring the earth. They were nearly squashed by falling trees. The roaring wind knocked them over and over again as they ran, pummeling them with flying rocks and debris. They did their best to dodge the falling trees and flying rocks as they ran. In the tumult it seemed as if the heavens themselves had become a monster, and this beast sought to destroy them with the full force of its might.

Finally, they saw the shack. When they arrived, the sight of their home was incomprehensible. Juna would not have believed it if he saw it, but the entire lake was being sucked up into the air. Waves of water crashed into the ground merely feet away from them. The sight was so awe inspiring that the prince froze where he was.

Trees were being uprooted from the ground while the lake's fish flew up from the water like upshot arrows. Bolts of lightning struck nearly everywhere in sight, striking the lake, exploding nearby trees, and charring the ground. Then, even amidst the cataclysm that was already tearing the world apart, the most awesome sight began. Like a giant finger pressing through the sky, a tunnel of clouds fell down from the sky on the other end of the lake.

The prince knew what it was but had never witnessed it. It was a twister, and it lived up to all of the terror that they were known for. The long dark funnel slowly fell from the sky and tore through the ground, making its way through the forest and sucking up the lake.

The prince suddenly felt a sting on his backside. At first, he thought it was a rock or stick, but when he turned he saw the newt biting him on the back of his pants. The prince was bewildered. He stared at him in shock. The newt was either chewing on his pants or trying to tear something out of his pocket.

The prince squinted and then noticed that the newt wasn't biting him. Instead, like a dog pulling on a rope, the newt was trying to pull him into the shack.

"Get in the shack, Your Highness! It's our only hope!" he screamed, pulling him towards the shack.

"You're right," the prince replied.

He made his way toward the door before he turned back toward the twister. Though he should've been more worried about his own safety, he suddenly felt a huge sense of grief. Odder still, it was not about his own life, but about their home. He stood in terrible awe over the destruction of their garden and lake.

He felt the bite again but was this time the newt yanked him into the shack.

"Come, Your Highness! Huddle in the corner!" he screamed.

They fell onto the floor and curled up under the cot.

The twister had avoided the shack directly, but it was pummeled nonetheless. Nearly a dozen times or more, the storm had sent large rocks and tree debris shooting through the house like cannonballs. Bolts of lightning struck so close to the house that they could smell the charred remnants of whatever it struck. In the middle of the day, they thought it had begun to rain at one point, but found out that it was lake water when they saw dying fish flop beside them. Instead of barrages of rain, waves of water slammed against the house like a battering ram.

The storm raged on that entire day. It was the most frightening experience that the prince had ever endured. The experience was more terrifying than the beast, the raging river, and the wolf combined. For the entirety of that day, the two were huddled in fear. Never had the prince known such dark feelings. Not only did he feel fear for his life and disappointment about losing their home, but he also had a deep feeling of helplessness, which may have been the worst of it all. Against the might of such a storm there was absolutely nothing he could do. There was no way to fight it, run from it, nor will the storm away. The only thing he could do was endure, and that was the worst part about it all.

They slept for a few hours at a time, but they survived the storm. They could not however, say the same for their home. They emerged from the shattered hut to find their home a mere wasteland. As if lapped up by some gigantic beast, the water from the lake was almost completely gone. Scores of dead fish and charred earth littered the ground where their beautiful lake had been. The garden of berries and nuts had been stripped from the ground. The shack was also torn to ribbons.

The prince walked along the lake's rim. He looked up and around at the trees that surrounded the lake. In the branches and on the ground, there were several lifeless bodies of the lake birds, song birds, squirrels, and rabbits. The sight of their corpses hit him like a blow to the stomach. He stared out at the now empty lake for a long time. He could not believe it, or perhaps he didn't want to believe it. Surely this had to be some nightmare he hoped.

But he knew it to be true. The newt stayed by him but said nothing, to which the prince was glad, for there were no words that could comfort him. The two walked back to the decimated shack.

Helpless to fight the tears, the prince dropped to his knees and wailed like a child. He screamed and tore at the grass as hot tears flowed down his face. He cried like this for a long time.

The prince had tried to think of what he could've done to prevent this, but nothing came to mind. There was nothing he could do about this or, even scarier still, there was nothing he could do to prevent this from happening again.

What about the future? he thought.

What would he do when he was the king? What would he do then, when so much would depend on him?

The answer was clear, nothing at all.

At last the prince stopped wailing, but he felt hollow. All of what he gained he'd lost. Throughout his wailing the newt had stayed beside the prince, comforting him by wrapping his tail around him and letting him hug his warm scaly body, but sometime in between the newt had left. Somehow the prince hadn't noticed when he left, but for now he was glad to be alone. There was no way the newt could understand what he was feeling or thinking. He alone would have the burden of being king. At some time in the future, he alone would have to deal with a crisis such as this, but for all he had learned and gained, he was at a loss.

For the first time he felt angry at the Hokmah. This was the time he needed a wise man, to make sense out of life when life didn't make sense at all.

Then a sobering thought came to him. *What could he possibly do?*, thought the prince. *For all his wisdom Hokmah is still just a man. There was nothing he could've done either.*

He decided to stop thinking and do his best to make camp. Juna found his canoe in the woods and made a makeshift bed out of it by placing leaves in its bottom. He made a camp fire and ate a few spare nuts from the ground.

Juna hovered around the fire, blankly looking at it. Now he was tired of being alone. He called out for the newt, but he didn't come. He was mad at the newt now. Juna didn't want to be alone with his thoughts. He wanted comfort and someone to ask questions to, even if the newt couldn't answer them. Hours passed, but the newt never came.

Alas, the prince put out his fire and went to bed.

The next morning the prince woke up just before dawn. Not really thinking about what he was doing, the prince walked toward the edge of the lake and stared out into the emptiness once more.

As it turned out, it was the perfect time to do so.

A few moments later the sun began rising from the horizon. It colored the sky with a beautiful auburn hue. It was odd to witness such beauty amidst so much wreckage, but somehow the sun made him feel better. The color and light intensified until finally the sun emerged above the horizon. Immediately the world lit up with light.

Sunlight rolled into the abyss that was the lake bed. The sunlight had turned it from a pit of darkness into a pool of starlight. The sight was very common, something he'd probably seen a thousand times over, but somehow it felt different now. What once was dark and lifeless, was now colorful and vibrant, though no life was there.

Then Juna thought he was seeing things.

Though he knew everything was destroyed, everywhere he looked seemed alive again. The lake wasn't there, and yet it was. It was even more vibrant and twice as large. He saw birds and bees in the sky again, fish jumping from the water, and forest creatures jumping in the bushes. He looked over to where the garden was, and he saw an image of an even greater garden, with bushes and tall trees of succulent fruit. He then turned to the shack. The shack nearby was not just fixed but built into a house.

He must be going mad. He rubbed his eyes and the images disappeared. For a moment his heart fell, but the strange vision kept flashing back to him. The new images were there, but not there at the same time, like a mirage of some sort. He knew it wasn't real, but felt . . .

. . . they could be.

"Yes, they could be," he muttered.

And the strangest thoughts came to him. They were strange not because they were mysterious or profound, but because they were so simple. In all his pondering the day before, he was looking for something deep, complex, or mystical to help him through this situation, but the actual answer was so simple it was ludicrous.

What once was . . . could be again, he thought.

The lake was destroyed, but he could always build it back. Unlike before, he knew how to do it this time. There was always more water in the river. He wouldn't starve. He could always grab some berries and nuts. Also, thanks to his prior struggles with fish, he had become an excellent fisherman. When he fished before he had to guess where to find them. Even when he did find them, he would sometimes fail to bring them in. Time, trial, and error had taught him how to make proper hooks, use the right baits, and look in the right spots. Over time it had become as easy as merely picking how much and what type of fish he wanted to bring home.

He looked around at the earth and something else popped out to him. The places where the lightning had scarred left little whiskers coming from up under the ground. He walked over and kicked over a burnt stump. The wood may have been charred, but the ground underneath still held roots. He scooped up the blackened earth and smelled it. It was obviously charred, but it had a faintly sweet smell to it. He rubbed it between his fingers and found it cool to the touch.

He dropped the earth to the ground and said to himself, "I'd bet the world that this burnt earth would make good farming soil. If not that, then it'd certainly be a good fire starter."

Juna looked around and a strange mix of feelings came to him. The destruction that had ensued was still there, but so too was the potential for all of the new ideas he had.

He looked out to the empty lake again. In a nearby tree he saw a songbird picking up sticks and taking them up into a tree. The bird added the sticks to a clump of dirt and moss at the base of a branch. From the way the bird moved and acted he guessed that the bird was building a nest.

And that's what he would do. It would be hard work, and there would be no guarantee that another storm would not come yet again to destroy his work again, but he vowed to remake his lake again.

He started as he had before, by digging smoother and deeper pockets into places where the lake bed had caved in. As he dug, the enormity of the task loomed in the back of his mind. When he dwelled on how much work it would be, an enormous urge to give up rose within him. The prince blocked out these thoughts. He focused instead on the task at hand and became lost in all the tiny details of his work.

He focused on the excitement of unfolding all of the ideas he had for the lake. He spent half of the day digging, then took a break to go fishing by the river. Since much of Juna's fishing equipment had been lost in the storm he now had to catch fish using a wooden spear. Because he had to fish by spear, fishing was harder than it was before. Nevertheless, he caught a handful of small fish and brought them back to roast them.

He was eating when he heard a familiar voice say, "I do hope you have a fish you can spare." He turned to see it was the newt. A flash of anger rose within him but died just as quickly.

"I sure do. Go ahead and take a couple. I'm nearly finished anyway," said Juna.

The newt snapped a couple fish into his mouth and sat beside him. They avoided eye contact with one another. They ate in silence for a few minutes.

Finally, the newt broke the silence.

Softly, he said, "I do hope you forgive me for being away when you were in such a state. After a while I guessed that you needed some time to yourself to . . . you know . . . gather your thoughts." He paused, reading Juna's response to see if his words were too forward. When Juna didn't react, he took it as a sign to continue. "In hindsight, I'm aware that you may have wanted otherwise. If that is the case, then I'm extremely sorry."

Juna said nothing for a moment. It was true he wanted some company by the end of his weeping, but in the beginning, he really did want to be alone. He couldn't blame the newt for his own emotions; he barely understood them himself.

"It's okay," he said. "I was a little mad at one point, but your thoughts were actually quite right. I think I did need some time alone. It hurt, but it helped me by the end. Though I must say it is very good to have you back."

The newt smiled a soft toothy grin. "I would say the same, Your Highness."

The prince perked up. "Besides, I've got some great ideas!"

The newt's tail began to flick. "You don't say! Well, what have you come up with?"

Juna proceeded to tell the newt about that morning and all of the new ideas he had for the lake. The newt became just as excited as the prince. They spent the rest of that evening bouncing ideas off one another and discussing how they'd unfold all they'd thought. They discussed and discussed until they had a plan. The next morning, they started digging and patching holes in the lake bed. The prince thought it was much easier to dig now with the newt digging alongside him.

The work itself was laborious and long, but their enthusiasm turned their tedious work into an exciting adventure. They took breaks to fish by the river, but each time they did the strangest thing would happen. Every time the prince lost energy or would try to relax, he'd look around and see the images again. As with the morning prior, the images were beautiful beyond belief. Before he knew it, he lost interest in relaxation and he'd jump right back into the work.

As they worked the funniest things began to happen. The prince, remembering the time it took for each task the first time, was constantly surprised how quickly things got finished this time. Within a few days the lakebed was finished.

They then began to fill up the lake using their bucket method, but while they did Juna came up with an idea. He looked down and noticed a puddle that was leaking water into another puddle. For some reason he began to play with the puddles using a nearby stick. He then noticed that the water trickled down from a higher puddle into a lower puddle. He looked at the river then thought of where the lake was.

Juna suddenly had the idea of building a canal from the river to the lake. Before they tried their idea, they tested their theory by digging little pools of water and making canals between them. After a couple tries they figured out what would make their idea work. After a day of planning they finally began working on the canal. It took a while to dig it, but when it was finished the canal filled the lake bed in the course of a day!

The next task was filling the lake with fish. Now that the prince didn't have his rod, this part of the job was harder. By using the spear, he couldn't bring back live fish. Bigger fish were off limits, too, unfortunately. This part of the rebuilding nearly stumped them. They remained puzzled until the prince sat down one day and found himself watching a spider make its web. He looked at the intricate lace of web and a thought about what spiders did. The web was like a net made of silk.

Then the word came screaming into his head.

"A net!" he shouted. "Let's make a net!"

And so, the two worked on creating a net. Just as the spider used a web to catch its prey, they would use a net to catch fish! They used several materials ranging from sticks and leaves to animal bones and sap. They came up with several different models which had several different effects. Some nets broke, while others caught nothing at all. Others caught only small fish, while others were suited for big fish. When they finally created a working model, they took note of each design and used them for the purposes they needed.

When they managed to catch fish regularly, another idea came to them. Instead of walking there and back each time they decided to meet each other halfway and pass the fish between one another. The prince would catch the fish and would meet the newt, and the newt would carry the fish back into the lake-well, the ones the newt didn't eat that is. After a while the lake was filled, and they progressed to adding the other creatures.

By using their new methods, it took less than a day to do so for the secondary creatures. Food at the ready, they proceeded to work on the new garden and shack. The newt dug rows of earth for the plants, and Juna planted them. Juna scooped up the charred earth and mixed it in with the soil. The shrubs and saplings grew so fast this time it made him laugh aloud to think of it. Remembering his idea about using the charred earth, he tried using the burnt wood for their fires as well. The charred wood was an instant fire starter and burned very long.

When the garden was stable, Juna worked on reconstructing the shack. Since Juna had never worked on construction before, the shack was the trickiest part of their renewing process. He did his best to remember how houses looked back in the kingdom and tried to think about what made them work.

He tried several things from simple huts, to a makeshift box-like structure, and so on. When those failed he took inspiration from the animals. He looked at how birds made nests, how the ants made their anthills, and how the rabbits made their dens. When they went to the river they saw a family of beavers working on a dam and Juna sat down to watch them. He drew several drawings in the dirt and on leaves. He came up with structures that had similar features to what was essential for a home. From what he saw, every creature had a home that had easy access and escape, a stable foundation, and concealment or protection from the weather. He knew there would be limits since he was in the woods and had no special equipment, but he felt he could build something that would do at least those things.

It took them a long while to come up with a working structure. On more than one occasion they nearly squashed themselves within their various structures. However, after a few weeks, Juna finally came up with a model that worked.

Even as things became more comfortable, the memory of Juna's encounter with the wolf never left him. Juna spent his spare time making weapons to protect himself. He made a bow and arrow, a few spears, and even a makeshift wooden knife to always keep with him. He and the newt made regular patrols around the edges of the lake to scare off scavenging predators. Whenever they ate, no matter how big a feast, they kept their surroundings clean.

Before they knew it, all was nearly like it was, or perhaps even better. They had food, water, and shelter at the ready, but that wasn't all. What made things better this time was the sense of security that came with the rebuilding. Even the threat of another storm didn't cause as much worry as before. Of course, it would be unfortunate to lose everything again, but knowing how to get everything back made him feel at ease. He felt as if the knowledge he'd gained was worth more than the actual things he attained or built. It was as if he knew the magic formula to life in the woods.

But even as things became better, a thought lingered in the back of the prince's mind. He didn't want to think about it, but he couldn't stop thinking about it.

It was about returning home.

The prince and the newt were eating a feast when the prince stopped eating and stared at the fire. The newt seemed to notice that the prince wasn't eating.

"What's wrong, Your Highness? You full already?" he asked, smiling. The newt swallowed his fish and grew more serious. "What's the matter, my friend? Has something gone wrong?"

The prince shook his head. "No, there's anything wrong really. In fact, things are perfect right now. It's just . . . "

The newt rotated his head. "It's just what?"

"Well . . . it's just that this has to end soon. As you know I've come all this way to learn from Hokmah, but it has been quite some time and he is not here. At first, I didn't mind it as much for we were focused on our lake. But now after everything is going well again, it makes me stop and think that he'll never come. I haven't said it aloud this whole time, but in the back of my mind I can't help but think he won't come. Perhaps he moved away, or worse even, has passed away. To make matter's worse, my father gave me a year's time to return and it's been nearly that long at least. Perhaps my father won't relent his title until I return, but at some point, I have to go back. But what will I tell him when I return? Knowing how to build a lake and survive in the wilderness isn't going to help me become a great king."

The newt frowned but said nothing. The prince did the same. Though Juna was right, they refrained from talking, because they knew it meant saying goodbye to one another.

There was a long silence, then the prince spoke softly. "The shame is that I've gotten used to being out here. It's going to be hard to leave the life we've created. It's going to be hard to leave . . . " The prince's voice trailed off.

"Yes, it will, my boy. I understand," the newt said.

"I don't suppose you might come with me. It'll be lots of fun. You could come back with me to the palace and . . . "

The newt cut him off. "I'm afraid there is no place for an oversized newt in the kingdom, my lad," said the newt solemnly.

The prince's face dropped. "Oh." He rubbed his feet through the dirt. "Well, I guess we'll be saying goodbye soon then."

The newt smiled, but it wasn't mirthful nor pitiful, instead it was a proud smile, the type of smile a father might have for his children. "Indeed, it is, but fret not, all things must come to an end in due time."

The prince tried to smile back, but it was too hard. He felt a part of himself break inside. He stared at the ground and focused on the dirt between his toes. Against his own wishes, he felt his eyes begin to moisten with tears.

The newt raised the prince's chin with his tail. He walked closer and looked deep into his eyes. Still smiling, he said, "I tell you what, my boy. Let us have one more day. I have something to show you come morning. Something that I believe you're indeed ready for. Pack your bags tonight for the travel home and meet me in the middle of the lake tomorrow."

"Why?" the prince asked. "What are we going to do?"

"Do not worry about that my boy. In fact, *do not worry about tomorrow, for tomorrow will worry about itself. Each day has enough trouble of its own,* you need not make yourself anxious by it. Now come let us clean up our meal and go to bed."

The prince nodded, though he was fighting back tears. Finally, he stood up. They cleaned their garbage and went to bed.

The next morning the prince did as he was asked and packed his belongings. When he walked outside he found the canoe placed precariously around the rim of the lake. He wondered if he should bring his new fishing gear. Perhaps they were going to fish in the lake before they left.

He reached around for his pack and heard, "You won't need that, son. Come as you are and all will be made clear."

It was the newt's voice, but it was faint and distant like an echo. It came from the middle of the lake, but he could not see him anywhere.

He did as he was asked and made his way out into the middle of the lake where he had never been before. When he neared the middle, he marveled at how big they had made it. He felt now as he had on the river when he had lost sight of the banks. As he paddled, the morning fog seemed to thicken around him. He looked around for the newt but still didn't see him.

"Mr. Newt. Mr. Newt, I'm here!" he called out, but the newt did not answer.

Maybe he is further along, thought the prince, but when he reached for his paddle something odd happened. There was humming noise vibrating through the water again. Juna's heart skipped a beat, for he knew that sound.

It was the sound of the beast.

"But there's no way it could make its way here," he muttered, thinking of the beast of the river.

Even as he said it the humming grew louder. A dark line appeared in the water. It rolled through the water, exactly as it had that night on the river. The prince's breath caught in his chest, for as unlikely as it was, he saw that the beast had somehow made its way into the lake. The line bent into a long circular pattern, almost like a coil, and circled the boat. Though the fog shrouded things the morning sun revealed enough about it to show that creature was something like a snake. The prince readied his bow and gritted his teeth. As soon as the creature rose its head out of the water, he would fire an arrow.

But as Juna readied himself for battle, the creature began to brighten as it did when he had neared the shore. The creature then began emanating the pleasant humming sound again. It was like a soothing ballad strum by a harp. The prince tried to keep his focus and his anger. He knew that however pleasant the sound was, the sound surely must be some tactic to lull or distract him. He predicted that the beast would then strike when his guard was down. The light on the surface of the water intensified into a brilliant silver that nearly blinded his eyes.

Finally, the creature burst forth from the surface of the water. It rose like a tall spire shooting forth from the earth. It rose higher and higher until it reached the height of the tallest buildings of the kingdom. When the prince could hardly see its end, the beast's head curled downward until it hung over him like a gigantic oak tree.

Juna raised his head to look at the gigantic beast and could barely believe his eyes. Though he had heard of them only through legends and stories, the creature before held all the traits of a dragon.

It was as long as twenty oak trees with the girth of ten oxen. It had bright silver scales along its body that glistened in the sunlight. A spiky spine ran along its back. Its head could make five of the canoes he was in and it had long whiskers that flowed outward from its nostrils as if they were the living embodiment of wind.

The prince was terrified and mesmerized at the same time, yet something about the creature seemed familiar. Its head was partially shrouded by the morning sun, but its body was visible. It had long claws along its forelimbs. He guessed its hind limbs were somewhere along where the creature's tail was, which was likely deep underwater. The newt had claws that looked like this creature's. The dragon was a silver color, almost like the skin color of the newt. The newt had the same color, but this wasn't the newt, it couldn't be. Yet the odd feeling of familiarity remained.

He looked up at its head. The longer he looked, the surer he was that the newt and this creature were related.

As if reading his thoughts, the creature lowered its head from the sunlight. The dragon revealed its sparkling white eyes. This time the creature's demeanor was placid. In fact, the creature was smiling, and not just any smile. The creature was smiling that same proud smile that the newt had worn the previous night.

The prince's eyes widened. At that moment he knew in his heart that the dragon before him was his friend Mr. Newt.

"But . . . but this can't be," stammered the prince. "Who are you? What are you?"

The dragon smiled and said. "As for the first question, I am a dear friend yet a distant stranger one in the same. As you may now realize, we are already well acquainted, but this part of my being has been hidden from you."

"You're Mr. Newt?" the prince asked, puzzled.

The dragon laughed softly. "Indeed, I am the being that you have called by that name. Yet I am not just a newt, my dear boy, but something more. Oddly enough, though you ask who I am, I can tell you that you already know my real name."

The prince was puzzled.

"I do?" Juna scratched his head. "My apologies, great beast sir, but I'm afraid I do not know your real name. Would I be so forward as to ask?"

A series of rumbles echoed through the creature's throat. The prince was startled, for a moment he thought he had offended it, but when he looked at its face he saw that it was chuckling.

"Hmph. Do you not know? If you need a hint, merely ask yourself on whose land do you now reside."

Juna was still confused, but then he thought about the shack. Then he thought about the letter on the door when he'd first arrived. After all this time he'd begun to think of this place as his own, but when he stopped to think about it, he remembered whose land this actually was.

The prince's eyes widened.

At last he realized what, or rather, who, this creature was.

"Hokmah!" he shouted.

The dragon nodded.

"Wow! This is amazing, sir! I am beside myself in shock . . . but how? My father said no mention of this. If you may be so gracious as to answer me, sir, what are you?"

"As I have said before, I am many things—a newt, a lizard, a great serpent, but chief most of all I am a teacher. I am appearing before you now because I deem it the right time to enlighten you of your instruction."

The prince's face scrunched together with worry. As eager as he was to learn from this famous teacher, he didn't have any more time to spare.

"Great teacher, I beg your forgiveness for my hastiness, but I haven't much time. Is there a way to postpone our instruction until a later point in time? Perhaps I could come back after I've told the king—"

Hokmah interjected. "That won't be needed, Your Highness, for your instruction has already been taught. Though you were not aware of it, I have been teaching you the principles of wisdom over the course of this year."

"You have?" asked the prince. "But how, sir? I have not taken any classes nor read any volumes of literature. Neither have I meditated nor contemplated over anything worthwhile. This entire time I've been merely surviving in the woods. Tell me, great teacher, how and when did you teach me? I surely do not feel wise."

Hokmah chuckled again. "Do not worry, my lad, for wisdom is not a feeling, nor do the wise boast of their insight. Wisdom is a quiet thing that is held in the mind and spirit. As for when and how I taught you, you merely have to look back over the course of this year."

The prince thought about the past year but could not recall what lessons he'd been taught.

"Oh, great teacher, please forgive me of my ignorance, but could you enlighten me which lessons I should've learned and tell me what they are."

"Why yes, my son, I surely will, but first you must take out your father's scroll and a quill, for any fool can listen to great knowledge, but *the wise collect it and meditate on it day and night.*"

The prince did as he was told and sat down in the boat. When he was ready he bowed to the serpent.

"Then let us proceed. There is an endless amount of wisdom that I could teach you, but these ten are the most important. Without them any other knowledge is useless. In another sense, you could call them laws, because disobedience to these lessons is the sure path to foolishness. Over the course of this year I have taught you ten lessons of wisdom over the course of ten critical events. Through overcoming each, you were taught of the merits of each principle. It might interest you to note however, that it was your father that instructed you in the first law. Think back to the beginning of this journey. Do you care to guess what it is?"

The prince knew this answer immediately, for his father's last words to him were what came to mind whenever he thought about his father.

"To do unto others as you would to yourself," said the prince.

Hokmah smiled. "Why indeed you are correct, Your Highness. The beginning of all wisdom for man is in his *compassion* for others. The lesson is important because in all things no matter how big or how small, there must be a balance. Obedience to this law is paramount for all other wisdom is moot without it. Never let your achievements surpass your humanity, for people care not how great you are until they know how greatly you care for them.

"To my delight, when I tested you in this you obeyed this lesson well. In fact, it was your obedience to this principle that began our journey together. When you found me and helped me, you portrayed care and concern for someone other than yourself. This is important because if everyone gives then no one is without. I knew that you would be in a hurry to find the home of the great Hokmah, so I tested how you would react if you were delayed from that goal. To my delight you not only took the rock off me but carried me to the pool at the expense of your time and effort. To this I would say, a job well done."

The prince blushed. "Thank you, great teacher. Is that all there is to the first law?"

"Almost. There is another part of that first law that you must not forget. Within that first law is an important idea called *reciprocity,* which means the maintenance of a proper relationship between two things.

"My response to your service portrayed this idea. When you helped me I in turn helped you by showing you to the shack. Undoubtedly, you must've felt that I was taking advantage of your kindness when I asked you to take me to the pond. I set it up that way so that you could also understand the wrongness in not also respecting the second part of this law. Do you remember what I said to you after you brought me into the pool?"

The prince nodded as he remembered the newt's insistence on his repayment for his deed. "I remember you saying something about paying me back for carrying you."

"In better words, I said to you *'it would be wrong of me not to give as I have received,"* Hokmah corrected. "In accordance to the law of compassion it is right to treat others fairly and justly. Never take more than you give for in doing this you break the balance of relationship. If a farmer sows a field but does not nourish the ground after the crop has bared its fruit, the ground will eventually wither, and the farmer will be without further bounty. It is in our nature to take and continue with our own concerns, but if you always remember to give as well as you receive you will never be without. This is the first law of wisdom. Now *write this down and seal it in your heart."*

The prince did as he was told and looked up to Hokmah. "Thank you, teacher. Can you please tell me what the second law of wisdom is?"

"The second law of wisdom is *patience.* You learned this law when you encountered my shack for the first time. The letter I left was a test to see if you were too hasty. While it frustrated you, I was relieved to see that you passed this test."

"Indeed, that was a tough test, your honor. If you do not mind me saying so, it was a very frustrating lesson to learn. I must ask, of all the laws why is patience the second?"

"Patience is second because it is crucial to gaining wisdom. As you may know already, knowledge and wisdom are alike, but not the same. Knowledge is anything that can be learned. We all take in different types of knowledge every day. It can be attained in short amounts of time and in longer amounts of time, but wisdom is different."

"How is wisdom different?" Juna asked. "Aren't great wise men very knowledgeable?"

"Why yes, they are, but it is not what they know, but how they use it. You see, wisdom is like making an elaborate dish. It has a definite process and method of creating it. No matter how good the ingredients one may have to make the dish, if one skips a step in preparing it, the dish is ruined, and its taste altered. Obtaining wisdom need not take a lifetime nor even a year, but it does require the patience to finish its definite process. In the case of our story you would not have been able to stay and learn the other laws if you had left in haste. Therefore, I had to see if you would stay before I taught you anything else, *for any lesson half learned is a lesson not learned at all.* When you made the resolution to stay no matter how long it would be before my return, you learned this second law. Now write this down and seal it in your heart."

The prince did as he was told then bowed again to the serpent.

"I will now tell you the third law, but to do so I must first ask you to take your bow into hand."

The prince shrugged for he did not see what a bow would teach him about wisdom. Despite his confusion, he obeyed and turned around for his bow. He picked it up, but it started to shift as if it were alive. He dropped the bow. When it landed on the ground it looked no different, but the prince could've sworn that the bow had moved when he touched it.

Hokmah's voice rumbled from behind him. "It is okay my son. Take the bow into your hand."

"I was going to but something strange just happened to my bow," Juna stammered.

"Trust me, my son, I know what happened. Have faith in me that what is happening to your bow will not harm you. Now do as I ask and pick up the bow." The prince hesitated. It felt like trying to pick up a snake by its tail. Nevertheless, he did as he was told and picked up the bow. As it had before the bow shifted in his hand. The wood became warm and shifted into a long pole with an oblong end. Juna could scarcely believe his eyes, but in a matter of moments his bow had become his shovel. The prince was surprised. He had left the shovel and all of the materials he had borrowed at the shack. He held the shovel in his hands and ran his fingers along the handle. This was indeed the shovel he had left behind.

He turned to Hokmah and said, "Great teacher, this is amazing! Was this your doing?"

The dragon nodded his head. "As a teacher I have found that students learn best when symbols are paired with a lesson. The shovel is a symbol of the next part of our story and furthermore to the third law of Wisdom. Now place one hand on the shovel's handle and the other on the spade."

Juna did as he was told. The shovel broke apart and shifted into two spherical objects within his two hands. In the hand that held the handle now held a small pitcher filled with water. In the hand holding the spade was now a clear empty vase. The prince was amazed; however, he wondered why the pitcher was full and the vase empty.

Am I supposed to pour the water into the vase? he wondered.

Hokmah began speaking again.

"I will now teach you the third law. This law is called *openness*. I showed you this law when you dug our pools. As it pertains to wisdom, this is the process of eliminating what you think you know in order for truth to fill its place. A full cup doesn't have room for wisdom, but an empty cup has room for wisdom to be poured in. The process of wisdom begins by making space in the mind for better information to come, for it is written *men do not put new wine into old wineskins, lest the skin break and spill it, but rather they put new wine into new wineskins so that the wine is preserved.*

"Now, as to our story I must bring our focus onto the actual work itself. Undoubtedly the chore of digging such a big pool was really hard work. Won't you say?"

The prince nodded. "Oh yes, great teacher. The effort made my limbs ache and burn for quite some time."

"Indeed, it should have been, for that work conditioned you for what later was to come. Without the strength you acquired from that task you would not have been able to do the rest. But just as the shovel, pitcher, and vase are symbols for understanding the third law. So, too, was the conditioning you were put through. Your conditioning was not the sole purpose of the digging. The true purpose of the painful physical work was to symbolize the mental pain one goes through when making room for better information. Throwing away our old notions can hurt our mental state, just as the digging ached your body. Often, we hold deep feeling toward what we have come to know and throwing it away can be quite hard, even if we know it is for the better. This is indeed a step that many do not choose to do because it is so hard. However, it is extremely necessary. Flat earth only holds water for a little while until the sun dries the earth again, but a pit holds water much longer. If you ever find yourself seeking more wisdom you have to first make room to hold it. Remember this and you'll always have more to gain. Now write this down and seal it in your heart."

The prince did as he was told and bowed to the serpent.

"Very well, my son, you are indeed a good listener. Now, as you likely put together when you saw what these objects were, I will ask you to pour the contents of the pitcher into the vase."

Juna grabbed the pitcher and poured it into the vase. To his surprise, the contents of the pitcher was a horrible looking substance that looked like tar or sludge. The contents also gave off a nauseating smell. The prince looked up to Hokmah for an explanation.

The dragon furrowed his brow. Apparently, he also found the substance unpleasant. "Hmm, that is rather distasteful isn't it?" The prince nodded. "Aye, as you now see, and smell unfortunately, it is very important what type of substance one pours into their mind. I'm showing this to you to introduce you to the fourth law."

Hokmah dropped his head near the boat. Like a living tree vine, one of his whiskers descended down and reached into the vase. The whisker touched the surface of the murky substance. At once the contents of the vase transformed into crystal clear water.

The dragon raised his head again and spoke. "Now pour out the contents of the vase and rinse it out with the lake water. Then pour in the new liquid from the pitcher. Also, do not worry about poisoning the lake or the wildlife, for no poison can dwell in the same water that I dwell in."

Juna did as he was told and rinsed out the vase. As Hokmah had said, the grotesque liquid disappeared as soon as it touched the water. When he felt the vase was clean, he poured in the new sparkling water.

"Good, my son, now we can proceed.

"The fourth law of wisdom is called *quality*. You learned this when we went to the river of living water. I urged you to get the living water because this too is also a key in becoming wise. Once you have made room for wisdom to enter your mind you must then screen the knowledge you receive. I have already told you that we receive plenty of knowledge each day. Be wary of the knowledge you receive and the people you keep in your company. It is written that *the one who walks in the counsel of the wicked shall find himself like the chaff that is blown away by the wind.* So too shall the one who *delights in truth will instead be like a firmly planted tree, bringing forth abundant fruit.* If that is true, then you should take every possible measure to take in as much *living water* as you can."

The prince thought about this for a moment and tried to compare this to his life. "But, great teacher, I am confused. How do I know what is 'the living water' and what is not?"

"That is a great question. For this isn't always easy to figure out. Ironically, truth often hides itself in even the darkest and trickiest of places. Nevertheless, here are a few hints.

"Hint number one: Stay away from gossip. The wise have a policy of saying publicly only what they would also say privately. If you have to say something about someone that you wouldn't say to them directly, do not say it at all, for with mankind *perception is reality.* Keep this in mind: small people talk about other people, but big people talk of ideas. It is written that *the mind is the standard of mankind.* Keep yourself in the circle of those who use their mind and are fascinated in the workings of knowledge.

"Hint number two: Learn from the learned. One of the most common mistakes of the novice is trying to learn solely from their experience, not knowing that those who've come before them have been in similar circumstances. The human expression calls this, 'trying to reinvent the wheel.' While every generation faces unique challenges that are specific to them. It also goes without saying that every human struggle has similar elements. It is written that *there is nothing new under the sun.* This is true, no matter the changing of the times. If you want to be prosperous in a way of life, ask the learned, wise, and accomplished in that area. Consult their writings and talk to them. In fact, this principle need not only be applied to certain trades or skills, but to any facet of life. Parents are oftentimes the best people to ask for guidance on matters of life in general. If one is young they should seek out the elderly and ask them to share their memories; the young cadet should go and talk to the seasoned veteran and imitate his ways. You'd be surprised at how willing most people are to share their insight, especially the truly wise. More often than not the wise love to share their insight with others for they know that *great knowledge isn't to be kept and stored but is meant to be passed on.*

"Hint number three: Learn the fundamentals. With any branch of knowledge, from science to literature, from arithmetic to art, there are basic and simple concepts that make them up. No matter how silly or simple these concepts seem to be, do not discount their importance. Think of the words 'elementary knowledge.' Surely the phrase itself should tell you it is important. Elementary knowledge allows you to know the elements of any problem, no matter how complex they are. If you find yourself stumped by something complex, go back to its roots and start over, undoubtedly the answer will come from there.

"However, if these hints confuse you, simply keep this in mind: Always be in pursuit of knowledge that betters instead of hinders and you will find that others will want to be around you. Now write this down and seal it in your heart."

The prince did yet again as he was told and then bowed to the serpent.

"Stemming from the fourth law is the fifth, the law of *progression.* Some people call this 'challenging oneself.' You learned this when we started to dine on fish. The morning you found that I had grown, you quickly deduced that bugs would not feed a large serpent like myself. Indeed, you were right in your thinking. So too does this apply to wisdom. As I have mentioned before, understanding elementary knowledge is vital for every path of learning. However, one does not become truly wise by staying in the realm of elementary knowledge. Any fool can pass an elementary test when they are at an adept level, but the wise subject themselves to challenge and the building upon what they know. Now take the vase and pitcher into your hands, for I have another symbol to show you."

The prince picked up the two items. As before the items began shifting in his hands. The pitcher in his right hand became a wide round and flat object. The new object formed a handle that fit along the back of his hand and wrist. In his left hand the vase had stretched into a long flat object with a pointed end. Both objects soon became heavy. In fact, in a matter of moments they became so heavy that Juna could not hold them up.

He dropped them on the boat, which caused it to teeter and sway. Once Juna regained his balance he looked down at the objects. He held a brilliant sword and shield. The sword was like the swords of Eskoloran soldiers, except this sword was bigger and longer. The shield also resembled the round shields of his kingdom, yet it was studded with iron rivets and made with a heavy thick metal.

No wonder I couldn't hold it, Juna thought, *the heaviest weapons I've ever used was a simple broadsword or spear. This thing is the size of a two-handed sword. And this shield is nearly as wide as I am tall!*

Juna guessed that he was supposed to pick up the items but waited to see what the Hokmah would say. He looked up to Hokmah, pointed his finger to the items, then pointed to himself.

Hokmah nodded. "Pick up the items before you."

Juna gulped but did as he was told and picked up the items. He tried a simple swipe with the sword, but it took all his might to swing. The effort nearly made him fall off the boat as it shifted when he swung. While he could pick them up, there was no way he could fight or move swiftly with them.

"Heavy are they not?" Hokmah asked. Juna nodded. Hokmah chuckled then said, "Well, perhaps these weapons are a bit much. Let me lighten that load for you."

At once the items changed into a wooden sword and shield. He tried the swing again and it glided through the air with ease.

"Now how do you feel?"

He twisted the sword in his hand, enjoying the ease, but feeling a tinge of guilt all the same. "Well, it's great that I can swing a wooden sword and all, but it wouldn't matter much in a real conflict. Real soldiers would use real swords and shields. To be honest, great teacher, I'm a bit embarrassed that I could not wield the first set properly."

The dragon shook his head. "Take no heed of that, Your Highness. I purposefully made the weapons heavier than you could carry so that you could better understand how progression works.

"Imagine the training of a soldier. A young soldier isn't given heavy armor to wear for he has not the strength to wear it. Instead he is given lighter garments and simple tools until he is stronger and wiser. When he becomes older and stronger he is then given the heavier armor because he is strong enough to wear them. But an older soldier is hindered if he continues to wear the lighter garments of his youth. He may be able to move faster because he is more than strong enough for the lighter gear he wears, but when he meets the enemy, clad in heavy armor, his ease of movement helps him little. Soon that foolish soldier finds himself cut down because he was not equipped to deal with the problems on his level. Of course, you could not wield such a heavy set of weapons at the start. You had not grown strong enough to wield them. If you had devoted several months or years to intense training with those weapons, then you would find these weapons as easy to use as that wooden sword and shield. In fact, with enough time and effort there is nearly no limit to how much stronger a person can become.

"But you went through your own progression during our time here. Recall your fishing experience in the beginning. As you fished did you find that the fishing became harder as it went?"

"Indeed, great teacher!" the prince said, nodding vigorously. "At first it was easy to catch fish, but everything seemed to go against me the more I fished. Every time there seemed either to be fewer fish or that they had learned my tricks. I had to change baits and fish in different spots. Even when they took the bait they fought harder and harder. I felt like as soon as I had gotten good at something, another thing would get worse. Tell me, oh great teacher, is acquiring wisdom always this way?"

Hokmah smiled serenely. In a soothing voice he said, "Aye. Indeed, it often is, but this is an essential process for acquiring wisdom. As we go on I hope you see why it is so hard to be truly wise. The path to it is tough and unceasing. But don't lose hope, like the digging did for your muscles, the tougher fishing also conditioned you. I bet you are a master fisherman now, are you not?"

The prince couldn't help but smile. He scratched the back of his head. "Yes, I have indeed become quite good at it."

The serpent chuckled again. "As uncomfortable as it seems, don't run away from this part of wisdom. It is punishing, yet just in its way. Just as the foolish soldier wears what is easiest, the foolish in general go toward the *path of least resistance*. Don't follow them on this path. It is written that *strait and narrow is the way, which leads to life*. This is the path of the wise. Despite how hard it is or how accomplished you become, always be willing to become a student yet again. Do this and you'll never see the face of pride. Now write this down and seal it in your heart."

The prince did as he was told then bowed to the serpent.

"We are getting along swimmingly. But first let me return to you what is rightfully yours. Take the sword and shield into your hand once more."

The prince picked up the weapons.

Hokmah's body began to vibrate and his eyes began to glow. The weapons began to merge into one another. They became long and slender until finally Juna beheld his bow again. The prince tugged on its string. Alas, it was the same as before.

Juna bowed once more. "Thank you."

Hokmah nodded. "You're very welcome, Your Highness. Now let us continue.

"The sixth law is called *variety*. You learned this law when we added the other creatures and fruit into our diet. As I have just mentioned, the path to gaining wisdom is often tiresome and tedious. Fortunately, the law of variety adds vibrancy and wonder onto this path by inspiring man to expand his views and interests.

"It is written that *those who become like children will enter heaven*. A child has a humble attitude toward learning because everything is new to him. A child eagerly soaks up all the knowledge that he or she can and is fascinated by nearly every intricacy they discover along the way. However, over time children lose that burning interest as what they learn becomes commonplace. Variety is important because it keeps man's mind fresh and stimulated. In a world as complex and diverse as our own, the man who finds himself with just one skill will be left behind."

The prince thought about this, but something didn't sound right to him. He was trying to meld this law in accordance with the other laws, but they just didn't seem to fit.

"But, great teacher, I am perplexed. I have heard it said that a jack of all trades is a master of nothing. If that is true, then how does the sixth law fit in?"

"I can see you think very deeply. That is a great question, for the saying is indeed right. It isn't wise to spread one's time and energies over too many interests. That path leads to exhaustion and ineffectiveness. However, recall what we have learned before. *Any lesson half learned is a lesson not learned at all.*

"The saying, 'jack of all and master of none', refers to one who uses this sixth law, without heeding to the previous five. The key word of the phrase is *mastery*. A *master* of anything hones his one skill until it can no longer be sharpened. Once this has been reached it is then beneficial to move off into another area.

"Despite the risk spreading oneself too widely, do not discount the importance of variety in wisdom. It is often the application of variety that brings great minds and peoples together. This is because great minds often tend to be in a variety of places. You would be astonished how often a remarkable thing is discovered from simply getting a different perspective. Remember this, a fool stares at what he knows, but a wise man blinks so that he may look at the same thing with fresh eyes. Never let your knowledge get stale for that gives way to arrogance and rigidity. Everything in life is connected. Truth never changes, but the forms in which it comes are always changing. If you welcome different outlooks, then arrogance will always be a stranger to you. Now write this down and seal it in your heart."

The prince did as he was told then bowed to the serpent. When he bowed this time, however, he heard a wolf's howl in the background. The prince turned to see a wolf sitting near the rim of the lake. The wolf was looking out toward the lake with a look of curiosity. Nevertheless, the prince grabbed his bow.

He was about to ready an arrow when Hokmah spoke. "You have no need for the bow, my son."

The prince turned to look at Hokmah. "What? Why not? Haven't we been running them off for many months now? I must run him off lest he linger here and attack me when I am unaware."

"I say again, do not worry," spoke the dragon, softly. "I have called the wolf here myself."

"What? For what reason?"

"For no other reason than to remind you of the next part of our story and the law that was taught through it. Can you recall what happened the first time you saw the wolf?"

The prince had no problem recalling his encounter with the wolf, for the memory was so startling he couldn't forget it if he tried. "Certainly, I can recall what happened. I was simply walking around the lake one morning when I came upon the wolf. When it saw me, it turned vicious and snapped at me! Luckily you came and saved me from it."

"Indeed. Now do you also recall what the wolf was doing before it snapped at you?" Hokmah asked.

The prince paused to think. He remembered the wolf sniffing or looking at something at the ground. As he thought he recalled the wolf was not just looking at the ground but was eating when he came upon it.

"Oh yes, I remember now! The wolf was eating some of the trash from our feast the night before. Perhaps that's why it snapped at me, for it feared me taking its food."

"Very astute of you, Your Highness. Now tell me what happened right after the wolf left."

"Well, we figured since the wolf was eating the scraps from our meal, we'd better clean up after ourselves lest we find ourselves in the same situation."

"Exactly, and that action is what I wanted you to learn from that encounter because this is in fact the seventh law of wisdom, the law of *maintenance*. It is written that *to whom much is given much is also required.* As you learned through that encounter with the wolf, a great gift requires care to continue to be at its best. The same goes for personal and practical wisdom. You learned from the sixth law that it is foolish to sit upon one's knowledge. For every great lesson learned, every lofty title achieved, and any talent acquired there must be a process of maintenance to keep it. It matters not if a great lesson is learned if it is forgotten the next day. The human phrase 'you either use it or you lose it' speaks of this law. Any fool can do something great once or twice in life, but a wise man can do so consistently for he has a *consistent relationship* with all that is important to him. In terms of abstract knowledge, it is always beneficial to go over its fundamental concepts and lessons. As I've said before of elementary knowledge, it is beneficial because it is the starting point upon which more complex knowledge is built upon.

"But the seventh law does not just reach into abstract knowledge, but to all functions of human life. A husband who isn't attentive and loving to his wife, may soon find himself without her. A garden that goes on unattended will eventually wither and become infested with weeds. And as for your case, Your Highness, a king who is not attentive to the workings of his kingdom and the people who serve him, will find himself supplanted from the throne. In whatever you do, learn, or are responsible for, be sure to keep a consistent relationship with it.

"A building without a solid foundation will implode under pressure and a tree without deep roots will fall upon the first harsh wind, but a man who is attentive to his work cannot fail. Now write this down and seal it in your heart."

The prince did yet again as he was asked. He looked out to the rim of the lake and saw the wolf was walking away. He had feared the wolf before that moment, but as he'd listened to what Hokmah said, he saw the wolf with new eyes. He thought it would be wise to still be wary of wolves for his own safety; however, when he thought about the lesson he learned from the wolf, he began to think of wolves as both ferocious and beautiful.

But as Juna finished writing down the seventh law something odd happened.

The world around him seemed to change. It was not as if anything had transformed or altered, but when the prince looked around, everything seemed to have become frozen in its place. The birds were suspended in mid-air and the fish in the water were stuck where they were. The prince began to panic but was halted by Hokmah.

"Fret not, my dear boy, for this is just an illustration to help us learn the eighth law. Please sit back down and relax."

The prince sat back down and relaxed a little but was still perplexed. "What is happening? How or what law could be illustrated by this, Great Teacher?"

"I have merely suspended things in time, all for the purpose of helping you see the eighth law. The eighth law is called *stillness*. You learned this when we chased down your back pack on the river. Look down at the water. What do you see?"

The prince did as he was told and looked. Nothing inside the lake had changed, but because everything was frozen he could see the lake in more detail. He could see glittering fish eggs embedded in the lake bottom. He could see small birds frozen in place mid-air. By the way they were positioned in the sky he could see that certain birds favored certain types of trees. He could see a film of insects coat the water's surface and fish just below the surface awaiting to gobble them up. Since the lake was sustainable, the creatures that lived in it had a way of life that made it not just a manmade water hole, but a living breathing ecosystem. This was the same feeling he'd had after the wind storm on the river.

As if reading his mind, Hokmah began to speak again. "What you are feeling is the effects of creating stillness in the mind. I set in motion the events on the river. When you first set out to grab the pack, the river was much too wild to grab it. It was only until later, when the winds had died, and the water was still that you were able to see not only the pack, but much more. Much like the sixth law, stillness gives vibrancy to what was once stale or overlooked. When the river was roaring you didn't have time to see all its little nuances, but, much like this moment, when the water was calm you noticed these nuances.

"As I have said before, everything is connected, but you can see this only when your mind is calm."

Juna nodded, but raised his hand in question. "But, Great Teacher, how do I become 'still', as you say."

"You indeed ask wise questions.

"Stillness is time taken away from the current of one's path to reflect, contemplate, or simply just 'exist'. Being still is not so much an action, nor is it the same as sleep. A good way to describe being still is refraining from any distinct action. This time of refraining from physical acts may seem pointless, but by stilling your mind, you give it rest and time to piece together the knowledge you receive. You are now aware of the vast amount of information we receive daily. So much as a man cannot stop a river from flowing, neither can any man's mind be at peace if he does not take time to rest. Take time daily to reflect or meditate. Being still can be as simple as taking time for a walk or bowing down to pray. There are multiple ways to reflect and meditate, but the key thing is this, *intentional time for your thoughts*. If you take time each day to become still you can remain afloat of all the currents in your life. Now write this down and seal it in your heart."

As Hokmah spoke, time unfroze. The fish and creatures in the water returned to their usual courses. The prince then became enamored with the fish. As soon as they were unfrozen, they darted through the water, becoming nearly invisible under the darkness of the lake. Juna looked at the surface of the water and noted how if one were to look only at its surface they could easily think nothing were in it. However, a creepy feeling rose within him the more he thought about it. He didn't know at first why this would cause such a disturbance within him. For some reason, the thought of something hidden underneath the water frightened him out of his wits.

He was nearly paralyzed with an increasing sense of dread but could not figure out the reason. It was as if something dark and monstrous was growing inside him.

Then the reason popped into his head. As soon as it did a question came screaming into his head. When he looked back up to the serpent he wondered why he had not asked it before.

"The beast!" exclaimed the prince. "If you were that beast from the river why did you attack me? I thought you were killed when you were cast into the river! What did that have to do with wisdom?"

Hokmah's face looked disgruntled, but not quite angry. He looked somewhere between conflicted and confused. The prince wondered what this meant. Perhaps he had spoken harshly, but he couldn't help himself. The more he thought about it, the angrier he got. He could not figure out why his friend would play such an awful trick on him.

"Out of all the questions you've asked so far. This may be yet the hardest one to answer."

"Why so?" said the prince, trying to calm his temper, but failing.

"You see, my attack on the river was designed to show you the ninth law of wisdom."

"And what is that?"

"The law of *temperance.*"

The prince went from incensed to puzzled. He knew what the word meant but could not understand what it had to do with why he was tricked or how temperance related to wisdom at all.

Hokmah saw the prince's puzzled face and began to speak.

"I apologize for my trickery, my dear boy, but do give me the chance to explain. It was never my intention to actually harm you. However, perhaps it is a good thing you feel angry because that indeed will help you understand the ninth law.

"Temperance is the ability to calm oneself amidst great anger or excitement. Like a molten sword quenched in cool water, so too must a person's temperament and emotions be cooled. Life presents to us a myriad of challenges, many of them calling for the best use of our knowledge and insight. An ill temper however can destroy any person's sensibilities. In a fit of rage or excitement, a man may ignore compassion, act without patience, or refuse to do the intricate processes that wisdom requires.

"Temperance refers to the proper relationship between the heart and mind. The heart and mind are two very important parts of the human being. The heart has the responsibility to feel, while the mind has the responsibility to think. Oddly enough, though their aims are often different, they are inextricably connected. One cannot exist without the other. I was determined to teach you temperance because, much like a lack of patience, an ill temper can destroy all you could ever hope to build."

The prince understood most of what Hokmah was saying, but he couldn't wrap his head around the attack.

"But, Great Teacher. Why the attack though? I have thought about this long and hard, but still cannot see how this connects. Please tell me why you attacked me and how it relates to temperance."

"Aye. You indeed deserve an explanation for such a fright. If you recall, I mentioned we were in the heart of the river before I was tossed. When in the middle of the river I changed into this form and attacked you viciously.

"I did this to show you how the heart and mind relate to one another in times of great excitement or danger. When we receive important information or are placed in a difficult circumstance, the heart and mind work desperately to influence the body. The nature of the mind is to contemplate and deduce over time, but the heart is prone to passion, which causes it to act rather quickly. It is important to note that neither faculty is better than the other. Deep contemplation at the wrong time can paralyze one's actions and cause greater harm than intended. Sometimes a quicker and more passionate move is needed in the times of crisis or danger.

"But . . ."

"In regard to making *wise* decisions, the heart is often more harmful than it is helpful. I attacked you in the heart of the river to show you that a person's first impulse is to act upon their feelings. This is one of the hallmarks of foolishness. The fool acts upon his passions before he has put them through the filter of reason and logic. Much like my assault upon you, this habit often causes harm to everyone involved. Like a raging beast hungry for flesh, the un-tempered mind is a dangerous one.

"When I attacked, at first, I thought you would merely freeze, or even more foolishly, try to fight back. Your response to the attack however, filled me with relief. Fortunately, you deduced that heading to the shore was your best bet for survival. While you were in the heart of the river I continued my attack, but when you got closer to the shore I lessened my assault."

"I think I'm starting to get it," the prince said. "But why did you lessen up when I got to the shore? What part of temperance did that illustrate?"

"I stopped attacking to encourage what you were doing. Through this I hoped to show you that getting to the shore is much like taking time out to think before one acts. If you had stayed and fought against a beast like me, you would've been harmed or worse. Sadly, that is what the fool chooses to do most of the time. They'd rather rage against the storm than find a hiding place. Surely you realize the folly in this. A man who tries to fight the authorities of his city will undoubtedly be cut down. It may give him pride to rebel and express his rage, but that pride is short lived. When he is outmatched and subsequently jailed he will curse himself for such rash thinking. This sort of thinking feeds one's ego, but often starves one's mind. It must've been embarrassing and miserable to flee to shore, but the wise often make decisions that are sound even at the cost of their own ego. Wise men make decisions that ultimately generate the most benefit, even if they feel wronged or angry. By swallowing your pride and using your brain you found the solution to your safety.

"As a leader of men there can be no more important quality than this. It is written that *if an enemy slaps your face, turn to him the other cheek.* If you can do what's right, even when you are wronged, then you possess the greatest strength of all. Now write this down and seal it in your heart."

Upon hearing this, the prince dropped all of his anger and bowed to the serpent once more. Once he had written it down he urged Hokmah, "Great Teacher, teach me the final law of wisdom."

"Indeed, I shall. But I must admit, much like the ninth law, it causes me great anguish to teach it. For I had to put you through great pain to teach it to you. In fact, the tenth law of wisdom is both the darkest and brightest lesson of them all."

The prince breathed in deeply then out again, calming himself for the words that were to come. "I am ready, Great Teacher. Teach me the final law."

"The tenth law of wisdom is called *humility.* You learned this after the great storm destroyed our home. Humility is the ability to humble oneself or purposefully reduce his or her sense of importance in the world. The common turn of phrase that represents this is 'being humbled' or having a 'humbling experience'. A humbling experience often puts man's ego into its proper place, and that proper place is not as master of the world, but as an important yet smaller part of a larger whole. The concept of humility is the hardest notion to grasp within the human mind, for it seems to go against man's great calling upon the Earth. While man is capable of many great things that no other creature can do, it is not entitled to anything under the sun. When a man first encounters humility it threatens him because it forces him to realize that despite his best efforts, tools, or abilities that there are many things that he cannot control.

"You learned that the hard way in the storm. To illustrate this to you I brought the most wicked storm imaginable upon us. I placed my protections over you of course, but I let the storm tear through everything you had strove so hard to build. Like my attack upon you in the river, I knew that you would realize that there was nothing you could do but hold on.

"It is written *that there are no things that are made that are not made in that way.* This speaks to the rigidness of truth and the unyielding nature of reality. No man can change the weather, the flow of time, nor even death. There are constants and forces that act upon the world without any say so on our part. The only option man has in the face of these forces is to apply them for his benefit or suffer through their misapplication. The forces of nature and reality belong to no one but themselves and they take only requests of man, not demands.

"Indeed, as I've prefaced, this is the hardest and darkest truth you must accept on the path to wisdom. It was an anguishing lesson to bring upon you, for I wept inwardly when you wept outwardly upon the ground. I am not sorry to teach it to you, for the law is what it is, but I am sorry for your dismay."

The prince thought about how he'd felt that day after the storm. Though he'd long since felt better, it still hurt when he thought of his despair in that moment. He looked up.

The morning was bright and beautiful, but he remembered the dark and gloomy clouds from that day. They seemed to hover over him now as the dragon spoke. As hard as the lesson had been, the prince knew that Hokmah was right. He had no power over death, nor the weather, nor even the whims of other people. He could not force the people to like him, nor accept him as their king. He could demand as such, but that didn't mean they would accept it. In his mind he could hear the words of the people who spoke ill of him. He imagined scenario after scenario in which people would ridicule him over this decision or another. The thought of such pressure quickened his pulse and made him queasy.

The prince did not think the teaching would be so exhausting to receive, but he soon felt heavy with the weight of each word spoken. He felt so heavy he believed his canoe would sink to the lake bottom.

In a pleading voice, Juna muttered, "So is that all there is? Is there any hope for man?"

Hokmah bent down until his head was merely feet away from Juna's. The prince could now see the dragon's face in full detail. With his large jaws and many scaly contours of skin, Hokmah was surely a fearsome creature to behold. Nevertheless, the dragon possessed a regal presence that exuded comfort and joy.

Hokmah began to smile and his large eyes sparkled like sunlight. He then spoke softly to the prince. "Why yes there is my son. This law is not a law that is meant to punish man, but rather is meant to teach him to understand the world that he lives in. It is written that *sorrow may endure for a night, but joy comes in the morning.* So too did you learn the brighter part of this same law the morning after the storm. And that lesson *is that there is always a choice.* In the face of all that man endures and experiences his only option is also his best option. A man cannot choose what happens to him, but he can choose how to react to it and how to think of it.

"That morning you learned that there was nothing you could do about what had past, but there were multiple things you could do for the future. As a king, and more importantly, as a man, there is no greater power you have than this.

"If you need any examples of this, call into the mind the rebuilding of our lake. Did we not discover new things along the way?"

Juna's face began to brighten as he said, "Yes, we did. It actually *was* easier the second time around because of all the stuff we figured out the first time."

"Indeed, and this is where the ten laws come together in harmony. By choosing to start again, knowing that you couldn't control some things, you discovered more, learned more, and enjoyed life more. It is a hard and tough world we live in, but by choosing to walk humbly within it man can go through great challenge or strife and still manage to love himself and the world.

"So, in your reign as king, no matter what happens, for good or ill, know that you will not be measured by what happens but by the choices you make afterward. If you let the previous nine laws guide your decisions, then wisdom will flow through you and onto anything you touch. Now write this final law and seal it in your heart forever."

The prince did as he was told, sealed the scroll, and put it into his pack. He stood and bowed to the serpent.

"Oh, Great Teacher, thanks so much for all you have taught me. I can't believe I learned so much and, even less so, how I learned it. I thank you deeply, for this past year has been the most memorable of my life. I will do my utmost to understand and apply every law you've taught me . . . but one thing still troubles me."

"And what is that, my boy?"

"Well, it's just that I'm still kind of scared. I feel wiser I guess, but I still don't know if I can rule as my father has."

Hokmah smiled a gentle smile. "To be quite honest, my boy, you won't rule like your father, for he is himself while you are yourself. Learn from him as you have from me, but don't expect to be exactly like him. When he came to me, he expressed the very same fear and dread that you have.

"Speaking truthfully, I can say that you likely will make some horrendous mistakes as a young king, just as you did out here. But when you despair over your choices, reach for the scroll, and remember the laws. Remember how you tried and failed at several things, but they all came to fruition by the end. Fear not your impending mistakes, but rather live in the dreams you will have for your kingdom. Just as you dreamed of a greater lake than before, dream of an even better kingdom than before and let not the mistakes along the way deter you from that dream.

"Go now, for you are plenty ready. Trust me in this and put my words to the test, you will struggle, but in that struggle, if you keep to the law, you will prosper in the end."

"I will, Mr. Newt. Thank you," said the prince, smiling.

The dragon smiled back at him warmly. "You're welcome, Your Highness."

They bowed to each other. Then Hokmah's body brightened again. A white light started to appear along the canal they built for the lake. Now, however, the water seemed to be receding from the lake into the canal instead of the other way around.

"What's going on?" asked the prince.

"Your swiftest route back home is through the river. As a parting gift I wanted to help you get home quicker. I will guide you along the canal toward your home. I think for all the trouble I've put you through that's the least I can do."

"It was no trouble at all, my friend."

"I am thankful that you say so. Now hold on tightly, for we ride at a dragon's pace."

And with that Hokmah dove back into the water and the current carried the prince up the canal. He looked back as the canoe traveled through the canal. Even as he went up the canal, the forest seemed to be holding them a farewell parade.

The birds that had lived nearby erupted from their nests and flew above him and around him. They sang joyous songs that filled the air with color and music.

The fish from the lake were swimming along the current. They sprang in midair beside his canoe, almost as if they were jumping for joy. Sunlight danced off their scales as they sprang up from the water and back again.

He looked to the sides and saw the woodland creatures running beside him. Everything from squirrels to chipmunks, foxes and rabbits were running and jumping through the forest beside him, all trying to keep pace with him in the canoe. Adding to his surprise he saw that the wolf was galloping aside the joyous marsh. Even as it ran it was joined by a pack of wolves. Fortunately, they looked as happy as all the other animals. Their faces were taut with big grins as their tongues hung out their mouth. They jumped over branches and frolicked through the forest alongside him. As they passed a curve in the canal they stood atop a large rock and began to howl. Their howls filled the air like a proud chorus of blaring trumpets.

All the while, Hokmah was underneath and beyond him, pulling the boat along with his spiny back. He had begun to hum the pleasant sound again. The joyous hum reverberated throughout the boat and made him feel truly happy. For all the forest had punished and beat him for the past year, it seemed now that the world itself was celebrating the completion of Juna's rite of passage.

Soon they had found themselves along the river, where the creatures began to taper off, but one creature remained with him the entire trip, the creature he would never forget for the rest of his life, Hokmah the Great Teacher of Wisdom.

Soon he found himself eyeing the brilliant towers and buildings of the kingdom. The current slowed as he neared a hill that overlooked the kingdom. He pulled the canoe over to the bank and climbed out. He gathered his gear, making sure the scroll was still safe and sound within it. Once he touched it to be sure it was there he turned, ready to say goodbye to his friend.

But when he turned, the canoe, as well as Hokmah were gone. A part of him sunk into the earth at that moment. He muttered, "Goodbye, my good friend, I'll think of you whenever I think at all."

And with that he breathed a deep breath and turned to walk toward home.

And so, began a new and brilliant age in the kingdom of Eskolar. As was promised to him, the prince was coroneted as king and he had a glorious reign for many years.

It wasn't easy at first, but Juna became a great king. As Hokmah had predicted, Juna made several mistakes in the beginning. There were many times where he wanted to throw away his crown, but every time he felt that way he remembered what Hokmah had told him.

He would calm himself and read the laws he had written down. Soon enough, through its application, he and his kingdom endured. No hardships, nor war, nor famine could tear him nor his kingdom apart.

Eventually, the kingdom of Eskolar rose to even greater prominence than under his father's reign. Guided by the laws of wisdom, King Juna became one of the finest monarchs the world had ever seen.

For more information about
R.C. Jones
&
The Prince of Wisdom

please visit:

www.facebook.com/R.C.JonesBooks
footballjones77@yahoo.com

For more information about
AMBASSADOR INTERNATIONAL
please visit:

www.ambassador-international.com
@AmbassadorIntl
www.facebook.com/AmbassadorIntl

If you enjoyed this book, please consider leaving us a review on
Amazon, Goodreads, or our website.

Made in the USA
Middletown, DE
10 February 2023

23813682R00050